PENGUIN BOOKS

2828

THE WEDDING PARTY

Born in 1905, H. E. Bates was educated at Kettering Grammar School and worked as a journalist before publishing his first book, *The Two Sisters*, when he was twenty. In the next fifteen years he won a distinguished reputation for his stories about English country life. In 1941, as 'Flying Officer X', he wrote his two famous books of short stories – *The Greatest People in the World* and *How Sleep the Brave* – which were followed in 1944 by *Fair Stood the Wind for France* (published in Penguins). These, and his subsequent novels of Burma, *The Purple Plain* and *The Jacaranda Tree*, and of India, *The Scarlet Sword*, stemming directly or indirectly from his war experience in the East, won him a new reputation and, apart from their success in Britain and America, have been translated into sixteen foreign languages. Of his later books, *Fair Stood the Wind for France*, *A Moment in Time* and four of his humorous books about the Larkin family are amongst those which are available in Penguins. His most recent book is *The Wild Cherry Tree* (1968).

H. E. Bates lives in Kent.

H. E. BATES

The Wedding Party

PENGUIN BOOKS

Penguin Books Ltd, Harmondsworth, Middlesex, England
Penguin Books Australia Ltd, Ringwood, Victoria, Australia

—

First published by Michael Joseph 1965
Published in Penguin Books 1969

—

Copyright © Evensford Productions Ltd, 1965

—

Made and printed in Great Britain by
Cox & Wyman Ltd,
London, Reading and Fakenham
Set in Monotype Garamond

Contents

The Winter Sound

MISS KINGSFORD had long been in the habit of keeping herself very much to herself; in that way there was no one to quarrel with.

The small white guest-house at the top of the cliff faced directly on to the sea, its wooden balconies shabby and scaly from much salt air. Many of the guests were old and frail. They moved slowly up and down stairs and in and out of thin-carpeted rooms like grey uncertain snails. A few also kept dogs; and since there was a large notice in the entrance lobby which said *All Dogs Must Be Carried* these few looked more like decrepit creeping nursemaids guiltily carrying with them shaggy infants, some wrapped in shawls.

By contrast Miss Kingsford, fiftyish, prided herself on really being quite young. She too kept a dog, a small grey poodle she had brought up to stare with disdain, even derision, at other dogs, so that he had become a kind of canine pharisee. Miss Kingsford, thin and neat and small and blue-eyed with skin as smooth as a balloon, looked not at all unlike a poodle herself, her hair carefully permed and tinted to the shade of pale-medium sherry. Her dog's disdain of other dogs had been directly inspired by her own disdain of other people, so that just as he was above the common company of lesser creatures she kept herself aloof from the dim affairs of snails and creeping nursemaids.

'Come along, darling pet. We mustn't loiter. Mummy will be very cross if you don't do as you're told.'

By the middle of September the summer visitors in the guest-house began to thin out a little, leaving behind mostly regular guests, of whom Miss Kingsford was one. But suddenly, wholly unexpectedly, towards the end of September, a Mr Willoughby appeared. And there were, Miss Kingsford was quick to notice, two exceptional things about Mr Willoughby.

The grey-haired, grey-eyed Mr Willoughby was neither snail nor nursemaid. He dressed with a certain air of smartness. His suit of thorn-proof tweed was of a shade of lichen green touched here and there with flecks of orange, with cap to match. A woollen tie of deep amber picked up the tips of orange to perfection and the same rich touch of gold shone from the highly polished brogues. Mr Willoughby was, Miss Kingsford thought, clearly distinguished. He was obviously, she told herself, not quite as other men.

Mr Willoughby was also well-mannered. In all her experience he was the only man ever to stand up in the lounge when a lady entered. It was an extraordinary experience, in a way quite thrilling, to see him rise politely to his feet at the entrance of even the slowest, dimmest female snail.

He was also, it was obvious, acutely shy. Every morning as Miss Kingsford exercised her dog along the wide grassy cliff-top Mr Willoughby fairly skimmed past her, head averted, to disappear into distances of gorse and tamarisk from which, some long time later, he scurried out again as if something unpleasant had frightened him there.

Always at these moments Miss Kingsford, who constantly kept her poodle on the leash for fear of having him contaminated or even sniffed at by other dogs, wished hopefully that Mr Willoughby would pause in his scurried passage and perhaps raise his cap to her or even offer a syllable of greeting. But for some days nothing of the sort ever happened or even looked like happening. Mr Willoughby always found some sudden path of retreat down the cliff face or over towards the town.

Suddenly one morning there emerged from the clumps of bushes not merely Mr Willoughby but two large, bounding, almost laughing Dalmatians. Unpleasantly joyful, they leapt wildly along the cliff-top, circled Miss Kingsford madly and then, as if intent on suicide, bounded over the cliff-top and disappeared.

A second later Miss Kingsford's poodle sprang into the air with the force of an electrified jack-in-the-box, broke from the leash and with toy-like barks of delight disappeared over the cliff-top too.

Miss Kingsford let out a sudden scream and Mr Willoughby, startled from shy retreat at last, came running.

'Oh! you wicked, wicked boy! Come back here! Come back! How *dare* you do that? Come back at once, I tell you! *At once!* —'

Even in this moment of crisis, when it seemed that Miss Kingsford might instantly burst into tears, Mr Willoughby was polite enough to raise his cap. In answer Miss Kingsford let out an incoherent shriek or two and then started to run with Mr Willoughby to the edge of the cliff-face.

'Oh! my God, he'll be killed. He'll surely kill himself —'

'Oh! no, no. Don't worry.' Mr Willoughby's voice was calm and very soft. 'There he is.'

Twenty-five feet down the cliff the poodle was standing on a ledge of chalk, tongue and tail intensely vibrant, looking down at the shore below, as if about to join the gay Dalmatians.

'Come back! Come back at once, I tell you! You naughty, naughty, wicked boy.'

'What do you call him?' Mr Willoughby said. 'What's his name?'

'Toff — Oh! you terrible, terrible, disobedient creature —'

'I think I'd better go down and get him,' Mr Willoughby said. 'Oh, it isn't difficult. Do you mind holding my cap?'

Why Mr Willougby should have asked her to hold his cap she never quite knew, but suddenly, without it, she thought he looked shyer than ever, oddly naked and unprotected. She began to tremble visibly as he climbed down the cliff-face, here and there dislodging a stone or two, and then all at once Mr Willoughby and the poodle became completely identified one with another. It was now not merely that the dog might be killed. A violent fear rushed through her that Mr Willoughby might be killed too.

A tuft of grass as big as a football suddenly dislodged itself from under Mr Willoughby's foothold and went bouncing past the poodle, startling it into another electrified jump that seemed about to take it down the cliff-face. Miss Kingsford managed to stifle a scream by biting at Mr Willoughby's cap but he, by contrast, seemed utterly calm.

'Toff boy, come on. Come along now. No more nonsense, boy. Toff – '

Mr Willoughby gave a low whistle and snapped his fingers. The poodle appeared almost to laugh. Then Mr Willoughby actually turned calmly round and said:

'The Dalmatians seem to have caused a bit of a stir. There's quite a crowd down there.'

'Oh! do take care.' Mr Willoughby was within four or five feet of the poodle now, crouching a little, in the attitude of stalking it. 'Do watch what you're doing.'

'Perfectly all right. Toff boy, come – come now.'

Perversely the poodle started to trot further down the cliff but in the same instant Mr Willoughby half-fell, half-jumped and caught him firmly in both hands, a moment later giving him a light but stern box on one ear. Whether from the shock of seeing her dog struck for the first time in his life or from the sheer violence of her relief at seeing him saved Miss Kingsford never quite knew, but suddenly cliff and sea and sky tilted and swayed in sickening confusion. A white veil of vertigo enshrouded her completely and then turned suddenly to black. A moment later she dropped to the grass, burying her face in Mr Willoughby's cap, smothered by a faint aroma of hair oil.

When she finally looked up again Mr Willoughby was sitting on the grass too, holding the dog in his lap. There was no heart in her to speak to the dog or even, at that moment, to Mr Willoughby. She simply gave the two figures a sickly stare.

'I think you'd better let me buy you a drink,' Mr Willoughby said. To her infinite astonishment he gave a short laugh. 'You look a little peaky. You won't be sick into my cap, will you?'

'Oh! my God. I'm sorry – '

Mr Willoughby stood up, gave her a hand and pulled her to her feet. She wanted to be sick but succeeded, somehow, in not being sick. Restlessly the poodle struggled in Mr Willoughby's arms and playfully he slapped its ear again.

'We'll get a sherry or a brandy or something at *The Mariner's Arms*,' he said. 'I sometimes drop in there.'

They started to walk slowly across the grass, Mr Willoughby carrying the poodle in one hand and his cap in the other.

'Why do you call him Toff?'

'What? – '

'Toff, it's an odd name for a dog.'

'Oh! yes – it's because he likes toffee. He always has two after lunch every day.' Suddenly she turned on the dog with quite savage vehemence. *'But we won't get them today, will we? No, we won't. Nor tomorrow. Nor the next day. Nor the next. We've been very, very wicked, haven't we?'* I've always trained him not to mix with other dogs. It was all because of those beastly Dalmatians. The coarse, common brutes.'

In the bar of *The Mariner's Arms* Mr Willoughby ordered a brandy for Miss Kingsford and half a pint of beer for himself. He had now tied the dog-leash to the leg of a chair and the poodle, cowed and quiet, crouched under the chair.

'What else do you feed him besides toffee?'

Miss Kingsford, sipping brandy, was quiet too.

'Oh! not so very much. I don't believe in giving them too much.'

'I suppose that's wise.'

'Yes. Have you a dog?'

'No. Not now. I had one once. But that's quite a time ago. Long before my wife died.'

The air above the sea was beautifully pellucid and Miss Kingsford, staring at it out of the bar window, was reminded of her moment of enshrouding vertigo.

'Oh! I was really frightened back there. When you – I'd never have forgiven myself.'

'Oh! no need to have worried.'

'But I *was* worried. Awfully.'

'And you? What about you? Do you feel better now?'

'Better now. Thank you for the brandy. In fact for everything! Oh! you were absolutely –'

After this the conversation lapsed inconclusively. Miss Kingsford again stared at the sea and Mr Willoughby at his beer. At last she said:

'What about the guest-house? How did you find it? Rather dull?'

'Oh! I've tried several along the coast. They're all much of a muchness.'

'I suppose so. Are you planning to stay?'

'I'm sort of looking round. Don't know where to drop my anchor. You're permanent, aren't you?'

'Yes, I'm permanent I'm afraid. It isn't that I – it's the best I can afford.'

Again the conversation drifted inconclusively and again Miss Kingsford stared at the sky above the sea.

'Wouldn't you like a dog? I mean, they're such company.'

'Not really. They're an awful tie.'

'Do you really think so? I think I'd die without one.'

'Mine was killed. Run over by a tractor of all things. It was pretty wretched at the time.'

'How dreadful for you.'

On the way back to the guest-house Miss Kingsford, just to keep the conversation going, said she was pretty sure it would be Shepherd's Pie for lunch. It always was on Tuesdays. That was the only thing – you pretty well knew what was coming every day.

'Do you rest after lunch?' he said.

'Yes, I rest. Do you?'

'I generally run out somewhere in the car. It passes an hour or so. I've been thinking of getting a caravan. I've given up my house.'

'I see.'

She gave Mr Willoughby a final smile of admiration, almost worship. 'And thank you so much again for all you did. It was really – '

For several mornings after that she missed the skimming figure of Mr Willoughby on the cliff-top. In the guest-house she noticed irritably that he seemed to avoid her. She never came down to breakfast. She took tea, with three digestive biscuits in her room. The poodle sat on the bed with her and lapped tea from a saucer and had three digestive biscuits too. At lunch Mr Willoughby read a paper-back propped up against a cruet. In the afternoons he disappeared somewhere in the car, not coming back until rather late for supper, when almost all the other guests had finished theirs.

Clumsily, one morning, the poodle tipped over the saucer of tea, staining the counterpane. In a moment of intense irritation Miss Kingsford cuffed it hard, scolding it furiously. The poodle crept under the bed and lay there silently.

'For that you shan't go walkies this morning. You clumsy creature. Into your basket! – in, in! – do as I say!'

Alone, Miss Kingsford walked along the cliff-top. A coldish, squally wind was blowing in from the sea. The air was bright and sharp and there was a touch of autumn in the air. She had luckily taken the precaution of putting on her fur coat and perhaps because of this Mr Willoughby, appearing suddenly from the clumps of gorse and tamarisk, didn't recognize her. Suddenly he was face to face with her, too late for retreat.

'Oh! it's you, Miss Kingsford. I – '

With his habitual shy courtesy he raised his cap to her. He seemed at a loss for further words and she said how cold it was. Oh! was it cold? he said. Yes, perhaps it was rather fresh.

'I'm glad I ran into you,' she suddenly said. More than anything, for days, she had wanted to run into Mr Willoughby. 'I sort of owe you an apology.'

'You do? I simply can't think – '

'Yes, it was awfully remiss of me the other morning. I never offered you a return drink. I really should have done. I suppose I was so upset.'

'Oh! that doesn't matter.'

Perhaps, she said, he might let her make up for that now? Perhaps they could go over to *The Mariner's Arms* and have something there? She really felt rather chilly anyway. She could do with something to warm her up.

Again, in the bar, Mr Willoughby ordered a modest half pint of beer. Miss Kingsford chose a sweet sherry and when it came it was much the colour of her hair. As she sipped it she said she did hope that autumn wasn't coming on too quickly. It was early to think of winter yet. Though it could be awfully nice in winter – bright, lovely days. Had he noticed you could see France this morning?

No, he said, he hadn't noticed.

'Oh! we often see it on these clear days.'

Once again Mr Willoughby seemed at a loss for words and suddenly she said:

'You seem very thoughtful.'

Did he? Well, it wasn't exactly that. He was rather puzzled about something, that was all. There was something different about her this morning, he thought, and he couldn't for the life of him think what it was.

'Me?' She felt her pulse quicken perceptibly. She looked him directly in the eyes. 'About me?'

'Yes, it's something – I don't know – Oh! yes, of course. How stupid of me. Of course – you haven't got your dog.'

A dark irritation ran quickly through her, quickening her pulse still further.

'Oh! don't talk about *him*.'

'Why, what's wrong?'

He had, she said, been very, very naughty again. Most tiresome. Really he'd never been quite the same since that business the other morning. He'd been so disobedient. And clumsy. She'd had to leave him at home. It was really too much.

'How old is he? Perhaps he's getting old.'

'No, it isn't that.'

Mr Willoughby sat very thoughtful again and then said at last:

'I've got an idea he really enjoyed that little episode.'

'Oh! you do? Then all I can say is he didn't deserve to.'

'He really laughed at me down there on the cliff.'

'Yes? Well, all I can say is I wasn't amused.'

Suddenly she felt that there was not only a coldness in the air but a certain chill between herself and Mr Willoughby.

'Oh! let's talk about something else. He really vexes me. Have you decided what you're going to do?'

Well, he had, sort of. Well, half and half. Yesterday he'd been to see a caravan. It belonged to an old friend of his. She didn't use it any longer. It was standing in an apple orchard. He could practically have it for free.

'And where is this?'

'Over in Sussex. It's really rather a lovely spot. Secluded but not actually isolated. Some rather nice woods. And there's a stream. I could very likely do some fishing.'

'Wouldn't you find it rather lonely? I mean, with winter –'

'Probably. But then that wouldn't be any change.'

The words penetrated her deeply. She was now at a loss for anything to say and drank at her sherry sharply.

'Anyway I haven't absolutely made up my mind. I'm going over to have another look this afternoon.'

'Oh! yes.'

Looking at her glass and seeing it almost empty he begged to be allowed to buy her another sherry. She quickly said no, she didn't think she would and then as abruptly changed her mind. He went over to the bar to give the order and came back rather nervously with another sherry and another glass of beer. A dribble of sherry spilled over the lip of the glass and ran on to the table as he set it down.

'Oh! I'm terribly sorry – I've spilt some.'

'Oh! don't worry. The glass was very full.'

'Clumsy of me all the same.'

He took a neatly folded handkerchief from his pocket and mopped up the few drops of sherry and then folded it just as neatly and put it back again. This meticulous little gesture affected her sharply, but still not as much as the words he uttered next.

'I don't suppose you'd care to run over with me? It's rather a pretty drive – '

'It's awfully kind of you.' Miss Kingsford felt warmly, uneasily thrilled. 'Do you really – '

'You have your rest and I'll be ready about three. Is that all right? It really isn't all that far and there's plenty of daylight still.'

After lunch she lay on the bed, eyes closed but sleepless. A recurrent vision of Mr Willoughby utterly alone in a caravan in an isolated, leafless orchard haunted her. It was wintertime; she saw snow on the ground and on the black apple branches. Once or twice the dog, toffee-less, still in disgrace, stirred in its basket and once she said:

'Don't fuss. We're not listening. Like it or not that's where you're going to stay.'

The drive into the country was, as Mr Willoughby said, very pretty. Whole woods of hornbeam were already turning a tender yellow. Fat port-wine berries hung heavily from all the hawthorns. Apples glowed from orchards like rosy-orange lanterns and a few late cream feathers of meadowsweet still flowered about the hedgerows.

'Rather nice country don't you think?'

'Yes, I suppose so. But I still prefer ours, back in Kent.'

'Really?'

'Yes, I always feel it's somehow sort of smug over here.'

Mr Willoughby drove the car at last into a valley of gentle slopes broken by strips of oak and hazel woodland and at the farthest end of it by an apple orchard of four or five acres still bright with unpicked fruit. A few sheep were grazing under the apple-trees. Mr Willoughby parked the car in a gateway and said:

'Well, here we are. Come over and see what you think of it.'

The trailer caravan, a green, light two-berth affair rather shabby and flaky, like the little guest-house, from wind and weather, stood in the farthest corner of the orchard, away from the road. When Mr Willoughby unlocked the door it instantly struck Miss Kingsford as being very poky. You couldn't swing a cat. There was a queer, musty, churchy smell in the air. It was sort of dead, she thought.

'I think it's quite homely in its way, don't you?' Mr Willoughby said. 'And you can just see the stream.'

Without answering Miss Kingsford peered about at bunks, cupboards, crockery, saucepans and a small shelf of books and then through the windows with their faded puce curtains at the stream flowing past, twenty yards away, between banks of alder trees.

'Well,' Mr Willoughby said. 'What's your impression?'

'Oh! I couldn't live here.' The tone of Miss Kingsford's voice was peremptory, almost irate. 'This would give me the willies.'

In his gentle fashion Mr Willoughby surprised her by saying that he wasn't, in fact, asking her to live there. He was the one who might be going to live there.

'I know, but you did ask my opinion.'

'Well, you're entitled to that, of course.'

'I thought you said it wasn't isolated.'

'I don't think it is. There's a pub and a post office and two shops a hundred yards down the road. I hardly call that isolated.'

'But in winter? What are you going to do in winter?'

He had not time to answer this before, from outside the caravan, a woman's voice suddenly called with pleasant breeziness:

'Ah! there you are, Charles. I thought I recognized the car.'

Miss Kingsford felt herself stiffen. She turned to see, standing just outside the doorway, a rather plump, fresh complexioned woman of fifty or so, her face well made-up, her brown hair without a trace of grey. A pair of drop pearl ear-rings gave her a certain gracious touch of distinction. She was clearly the sort of person who smiled almost perpetually and her silk green and purple dress was cut rather low.

'Oh! Charles, I'm sorry, I didn't realize you had someone with you. But how nice to see you again so soon.'

With his customary politeness Mr Willoughby stepped outside the caravan and greeted her with a light kiss on both cheeks. This was clearly what she expected and Miss Kingsford held herself coldly, silently aloof.

'Miss Kingsford, may I introduce Mrs Arbuthnot? An old friend of mine.'

Miss Kingsford, he explained, was staying at the guest-house. Mrs Arbuthnot came forward and shook hands with Miss Kingsford. Her hand was warm. Her face flowered with an unbroken, expansive smile.

'Charles, do forgive me for intruding like this. I'd really no idea you'd brought someone with you.'

'Oh! please don't mind me,' Miss Kingsford said.

'I was going to drop you a line,' Mr Willoughby said, 'and then I thought I'd like to run over once more before I finally made up my mind.'

'And have you made up your mind?'

'Well, there would have to be one condition.'

'Oh! really, what?'

'I should have to insist on paying some sort of rent.'

'Oh! nonsense. You know I wouldn't dream of it. Here the thing stands. I never use it.'

'Well, it's very sweet of you. But just a peppercorn.'

'Oh! very well, then. Just a peppercorn.'

Mrs Arbuthnot smiled even more expansively and a moment later Miss Kingsford broke in on the intimacy of the conversation by saying:

'I'm sure you two have business to talk over. Do you mind if I walk as far as the stream?'

'Oh! won't you come over to the house for a cup of tea? Do. It's only two minutes – '

'Well, thank you, but I should really like to get back. I've got one or two bits of shopping to do before they close.'

Miss Kingsford walked away to the stream. She stood on the bank and stared at it bleakly. It really wasn't, she thought, much of a stream and suddenly she knew she hated the caravan. Twenty yards away a solitary moorhen, disturbed, suddenly plopped sharply into the water and a moment later the sound was echoed and expanded by a long and gracious peal of Mrs Arbuthnot's laughter. When it finally died she even heard Mr Willoughby laughing too.

Under the impulse of these sounds she walked away up the stream. She walked for two hundred yards or so, until a fence prevented her walking any further. Then, for quite how long she didn't quite know, she leaned on the fence and stared into the stream, once or twice hearing, even at that distance, fresh peals of Mrs Arbuthnot's laughter.

When she finally walked back to the caravan Mr Willoughby advanced to meet her and said:

'Ah! there you are. We'd almost begun to think we'd lost you.'

'Oh! don't worry. I'm not easily lost.'

With gracious ease Mrs Arbuthnot shook hands and said good-bye. She was sorry Miss Kingsford wouldn't stay for tea. She hoped she would come again some other time. In farewell to Mr Willoughby she offered both cheeks and Mr Willoughby kissed them politely.

'Well, we'll be in touch – '

In the car, after an awkward silence of some ten minutes or so, Miss Kingsford said:

'Well, are you going to take it?'

'Yes. I think so. It's what I've been looking for. I'm sorry you didn't like it.'

'Oh! it's nothing to do with me.'

Another long awkward silence followed and they were

almost within sight of the coast again before Mr Willoughby said:

'Of course I shall entirely repaint the thing. And it needs a new cooker. And Mrs Arbuthnot's promised to make some fresh curtains. She's such a friendly person.'

Too friendly, Miss Kingsford wanted to say, but offered nothing but bleak silence in answer.

'You'd never think she suffered the most ghastly tragedy a few months back. Her father and husband were driving down late one night from town. The car hit a tree – '

'Oh! I see.'

'She simply refuses to let it get her down. She's always the same. So buoyant and gay. It's quite inspiring.'

'Yes,' Miss Kingsford said. 'I suppose she'll make a good neighbour.'

A week later Mr Willoughby left the guest-house. Miss Kingsford, determined not to say good-bye, stayed in her room all day, keeping herself, after her habit, very much to herself. But when darkness fell she put on her fur coat and walked along the cliff-top, with the dog for company.

Half way along the cliff-top she unleashed the poodle and let him run. At the place where he had once raced over the cliff and she had feared Mr Willoughby might kill himself she halted and stood looking down. A cold wind was blowing and she could hear breakers beating on the shore. Then she thought she heard the dog whine in the darkness and presently it seemed as if the separate sounds of wind and dog and breakers were woven into one long continuous sound. And after a time she knew there was no mistaking that sound.

It was the sound of winter.

The Wedding Party

MIKE HILLYARD stood on the terrace of the hotel leaning on a long stone balustrade under which big beds of scarlet salvia were fiery in the thunder gloom of late afternoon, idly watching the lake and the mountains beyond.

A mountain shaped exactly like a sugar cone rose from straight across the water, wreathed at the very top with a grey halo of cloud. From the foot of it, every minute or so, storm signals darted out like orange soundless fireworks. The gloom was almost purple, the lake water momentarily iridescent where low light from breaking cloud struck it. Far off, a solitary slip of sunlight caught a single low alpine meadow and turned it into a flag of such luminous emerald brilliance that it too might have been some sort of signal to the opposite shore. Behind the hotel the tempestuous rain of early afternoon had turned a mountain stream into a ferocious white-green torrent that he could hear crashing down its many waterfall steps like a continuous echo of the earlier thunder.

Suddenly, from behind a high perpendicular crag of rock, a steamer slid into sight, a gigantic snow-white swan dressed with many-coloured bunting. As it came nearer he could just hear from it, above the noise of the waterfall, the sound of someone playing a guitar and then of people singing.

Even more suddenly the steamer performed a strange miracle. It laid on the water a vast clutch of eggs, a hundred or more in pink and blue and green and scarlet and mauve. As they floated and bobbed and spread in its wake a boat propelled by two boys in blue swimming trunks darted out from the shore, followed by another and another until there were half a dozen of them, chasing joyfully the stream of retreating balloons.

On the bridge of the steamer the figure of a heavy man in

morning dress appeared, a bright red rose in his buttonhole, a waving champagne bottle in one hand: a figure gross and gay, shouting stentorian nothings to the shore. Presently it was joined by two others, also bearing bottles, and this tipsy brotherhood of triplets began to sing, in German, some loud bellying song.

Below, on deck, cameras flashed and many people were dancing: the men florid, the women gay and flowery, some wearing fur wraps against the cooling evening air. In the saloon a vast quantity of food was spread out on white-clothed tables jewelled with half-empty glasses, wine bottles and pyramids of pink and yellow roses.

On the bridge a tipsy hand pulled at a cord and for fully half a minute the blast of the steamer's siren completely drowned the chatter of voices, the sound of the guitar, the waterfall and the wild stentorian song.

A moment or two later the steamer bumped against the jetty piles. Two gangways rattled across to the landing stage. A laughing menagerie of passengers emerged, more cameras flashing, the men like so many penguins, among them all a young bride in a cream lace head-dress, carrying a bouquet of white and yellow roses. She stood there for some moments looking slightly bewildered, even forlorn until at last she was joined by the man of stentorian voice from the bridge, still carrying the champagne bottle in his hand. In the final moment as she took his arm another rasping blast from the steamer's siren split the air, the long repetition of its echoes talking its way across the mountains until finally lost somewhere far away in cloud-hidden snows.

Hillyard suddenly found the frock-coated concierge of the hotel at his side.

'A gay scene,' Hillyard said.

'A big, important wedding, sir. The daughter of a big business man. Manufacturer of soap. Did you not see the steamer when it left earlier in the afternoon, sir?'

'No, I didn't see it. I went for a walk in the woods this afternoon. Where has the steamer been?'

'Oh! simply for a tour of the lake, sir. For eating and drinking and dancing and making a good time.'

'And now what happens?'

'Oh! more eating and drinking and dancing, sir. More good times. More fun. Excuse me now, sir – '

Alone again, Hillyard watched the last of the passengers leave the steamer. As they came ashore he was suddenly struck by the fact that a fair-haired girl in a deep green and purple dress was the only one among them not laughing. She momentarily hestitated half way across the gangway, looked back, seemed as if she had forgotten something and then suddenly looked up at him and held him for a fraction of a minute in a steady stare.

For a second or two he was half-tempted to smile back at her. But there was no hint of invitation on her face: only the stare that might have been appealing, slightly resentful or merely curious. He couldn't tell at all and a moment later she moved on, crossed the landing stage, all alone, and disappeared.

A white-coated platoon of waiters now began to bear impossible masses of uneaten food from the steamer: vast platters of cold salmon, cold sucking pigs, roast turkeys, fiery lobsters, great boulders of brown-red beef. At one stage some extravagant piece of iced confection conjured into the shape of a much-turreted *Schloss* appeared, all pink and soap-like itself, that took the strength of two waiters to carry away. Lavish baths of fresh strawberries followed, drowned in cream, and finally a great coloured cornucopia of fruit, shaped like a gold canoe, that needed the strength of four men.

As the last of the drifting balloons floated away across the lake like tiny waning moons in the growing gloom of evening, he turned and went into the hotel. It was time for a drink, he thought, and started to make his way to the bar. It was a very nice bar, cool and roomy, with pleasant green tanks of tropical fish set about the walls, and it was his favourite habit to sit there for an hour every evening and drink a glass or two of hock and read or write post-cards.

Now as he went upstairs to it he was suddenly assailed by the amplified shrieks of a parrot-house. The wedding menagerie had taken over.

He was first annoyed, then abruptly, hotly angry. He turned with intense impatience and, not looking where he was going, started to go back downstairs. Half way down he managed to avoid a collision with a man escorting a dark-haired girl upstairs and then, a moment later, actually struck with his elbow a second girl coming slowly up behind, half-swivelling her against the wall.

For the second time the girl in the green and purple dress held him in that half-accusatory, half-appealing stare.

'I am most terribly, terribly sorry,' he said.

'It is quite all right.'

'It was very clumsy of me. I do apologize. I wasn't looking where I was going.'

'There is no need. I wasn't looking where I was going either.'

He stook awkward and embarrassed. He hoped she would smile but she gave, for the second time, no hint of a smile.

'Please,' he said and suddenly stood aside to let her pass. 'I'm sorry. You want to get to your party.'

This time she did smile, but with the merest twist of her lips.

'Why should you think I want to get to the party?'

'I simply – don't you?'

'No.'

'Not really? After someone has taken so much trouble?'

'Oh! yes, someone has taken a great deal of trouble.'

All this time he had been struck by the excellence of her English and now said:

'Your English is exceptionally good. Have you been to England?'

'No.'

'You have hardly any accent at all.'

'My education was a very expensive one.'

He stood aside to let another couple pass upstairs. The

man gave a short formal bow but the girl in the green and purple dress made no movement in answer.

At this moment he had half a mind to beg her to excuse him and take his leave, but she said:

'And where were you going in such a great hurry?'

He explained about the bar. 'And then the menagerie – ' The word slipped out before he could stop it.

'The what? Oh! yes the menagerie. The wild animals. That's good.'

Now she lifted her head slightly, in an attitude of listening, the twist of her lips very slightly cynical, and it might have been that she was listening to the sound of the menagerie for the first time. Then she said:

'If it was a drink you wanted the *Stube* behind the hotel is nice. It's very quiet there.'

'I know. I go there sometimes for a change. They have a very good Niersteiner there.'

'Ah! you like Niersteiner?' She smiled again, but pleasantly now. 'I like Niersteiner too.'

A few minutes later they were sitting on the bare, simple wooden settles of the *Stube*.

'And who is being married today?'

At first she didn't answer. For fully half a minute she sat staring into her glass. The wine, frosty, pale green, had arrived in big deep glasses, almost goblets, and she might have been staring into the depths of a well. At last she said:

'My sister. The youngest one. Trüdi.'

He was about to ask the troublesome question as to why she didn't want to go to the party when he suddenly remembered that sometimes girls, driven by resentment, jealousy, or mere pique, act in the strangest fashion on their sisters' wedding days. It might even have been, he thought, that she was wearing the dark green dress out of sheer obstinacy or perhaps the desire for a little limelight too.

Instead of speaking he sipped at his wine and looked at her, first at her bare arms, then at her face. Her skin was shining, golden and incredibly smooth. The arms were quite hairless. Her very light yellow hair was very smooth too and she wore it piled up, the effect being to make her seem taller than she really was. Her eyes were an extraordinarily pale transparent blue and reminded him very much of a big-belled campanula he had seen growing high up between the lake and the snows.

Suddenly she said, rather absently:

'What is that sound I can hear all the time?'

'Oh! that? The waterfalls. There are nine or ten of them.'

'Oh! yes, of course. I remember now.'

'Do you know the valley up there? I walk up there every day. It's a favourite walk of mine. For a time it's all crash and bang and excitement with the water rushing down and then gradually it's wonderfully quiet. Absolutely still. Nothing but trees and masses of meadow flowers and crowds of butterflies.'

She laughed. 'Just like getting away from the menagerie.'

'Just like that.'

She drank rather deeply at her wine, said how good she thought it was and then asked:

'How long have you been here?'

'Ten days.'

'And after this? Back to England?'

He said no, he didn't think so. He thought of going first to Salzburg, then Vienna and then, at the very last, to Venice.

'Venice.'

'You know it?'

'I'm afraid not.'

'All that expensive education but no Venice.'

'It was a very dull education.' She again gave him that brief, rather twisted smile. 'Excitements like Venice were not in the curriculum.'

'Yes, it's exciting, Venice.'

'I always wanted to go there.'

By now it was getting dark. Already lights were on in the *Stube* and now they also began to come on in the street outside. Little chains of them began to break out on the hillsides.

He then noticed that her glass was almost empty. He at once said he would order more wine – that was unless she felt she should get back to the party now?

'Are you so anxious I should get back to the party?'

'No. It wasn't that. It was just that I thought they might think it odd – '

'They know how I feel.'

He ordered more wine. It came again in the big goblet-like glasses. He picked up his, raised it, looking straight at her, and said:

'Well, since you are not going to the party may I at least toast the bride and bridegroom?'

'The bride, but not the bridegroom.'

So this, he said, was the reason for it all?

'Partly. But it isn't quite so simple as that.'

He now recalled the image of the bridegroom: the gay, gross, champagne-waving German of stentorian voice, part of the coarse triplet brotherhood on the bridge of the steamer.

'So it's him you don't like? I could understand that – '

'Like him? Heinrich? That monster? God above, I hate him.' A flurry of anger rushed through her face; the restless eyes actually seemed to darken a shade or two, quite bruised. 'Oh! for Heaven's sake don't let's talk about it. Let's talk about something decent. Those butterflies or something. Are you very fond of that sort of thing? – butterflies – flowers – '

'I'm sorry I spoke about the bridegroom. I apologize. I didn't intend to upset you.'

'Oh! please don't keep apologizing.'

He sipped, in silence, at his wine. He suddenly felt the intrusion on her privacy, painful as it was, to be far more of an embarrassment to himself than to her. He felt caught in a deadlock, wretched, completely at a loss for anything to say, but a moment later she gave the most embalming of smiles, quite without bitterness, and said:

'"Never speak to strange men," my English governess used to say. No good can ever come of it. But it isn't always quite true, is it? It's been a great comfort to talk to you.'

He laughed and sipped at his wine. 'When I came out of that bar I didn't exactly see myself in the role of comforter.'

'Well, here you are anyway.'

As she said this she leaned forward, put her arms on the table and looked him quietly full in the face. For a second or two he caught sight of the shadow between her breasts. Against the dark green-and-purple of her dress the skin of the upper curves of them looked paler than ever.

For some time after that they sat without talking, simply sipping wine and looking at each other. All the time he felt a gentle tension building up inside himself, whereas she, by contrast, seemed to grow a little more calm, the cynical restlessness dropping away.

It was she who broke the silence at last by saying:

'I don't think I've ever met a man before who was interested in butterflies.'

'Oh! I just like them, that's all.'

'I think you're a sensitive person. By the way, what is your name?'

He told her. 'Mike. And you?'

'Heidi.'

A quick spasm of hunger, kindled by the wine, suddenly rippled through him.

'Would you care to have something to eat?' he said. 'They serve a few things here. Or couldn't you face it after that feast on the steamer?'

'I didn't eat much. Yes: perhaps a sandwich would be nice.'

'I'll call the girl.'

Then she said: 'And afterwards perhaps we might walk a little way and listen to the waterfalls?'

'I hate to bring up the subject of the party again,' he said, 'but are you really not going back?'

'Really not.'

'In that case I've got a better idea. We'll ask the girl to pack the sandwiches and I'll buy a bottle of Niersteiner and borrow some glasses. It's such a warm evening. There's a hut up there.'

For some distance up the path going up by the waterfall there were lights at intervals but beyond the last of the houses and the wooden cattle barns the steep little valley was all darkness except for a great spread of summer stars and the candescent flash of the thundering falls.

As the sound of the falls finally died away a great silence clenched itself on the hillside, broken only by an occasional plop! of water falling from a bough in woods still drenched with rain. In that profound singing silence he stopped once and said:

'Do you notice anything strange?'

'No. I don't think so. What?'

'You can't hear the water any more. You see, the stream comes out of the mountainside.'

The hut was no more than an open wooden shelter. The air was damp and warm and sharp with the odour of pines. The sandwiches, of ham and *Leberwurst*, were laid on thick open panels of half-dark bread.

'Venice. Tell me about Venice.'

He talked for a time about Venice. It was always about to change, everyone was always telling you, but really it never did. Since the war he had been there half a dozen times and really it hardly changed at all. He told her of an island, across the lagoon, where a big old *trattoria*, cool as a cellar, sat in a garden of vines, oleanders and pomegranate trees. You could eat in the shade of great walnut trees and drink ice-cold wine with peaches floating in it.

'That sounds exciting.'

'It is. Why don't you go and see it for yourself?'

'I! – '

'With me, I mean. I'd go tomorrow if – '

She gave a positive crow of laughter.

'We meet on the hotel staircase. Total strangers. You English, I German. And in ten minutes you are asking me to run away with you.'

'And why not?'

'Eat your sandwich. You said how hungry you were. And do be sensible.'

'I am very, very, sensible.'

Below them lights ringed the lake in a series of irregular necklaces. The air had cleared itself of cloud. On the summit of the sugar-cone mountain a light burned like a crimson-yellow star.

'I wish now we'd brought two bottles of wine,' he said. 'It's so good.'

Again she gave that high crow of laughter.

'There you go again. One bottle takes us to Venice,' she said and once again she laughed, 'and where do we go with two? Heavens, how right my governess was – '

He was about to say that he liked to hear her laugh when suddenly, for some reason, it struck him that she was laughing too much and that the laughter, perhaps, wasn't as joyful as it seemed.

'Oh! there are plenty of places – Good God!' He suddenly leapt to his feet. 'Look! – your steamer's sailing. It's going without you. Now what do you do?'

'Oh! yes, I know.' She was quite unmoved. 'It's going home to bed. There will be cars to pick us up in the morning.'

He sat down again, watching the lights of the steamer as she drifted down the lake and remembering at the same time that impossible, gargantuan feast of food.

'I suppose the day has been a little expensive for your father.'

Immediately she became very quiet. It was too dark in the hut to see the expression on her face but suddenly he sensed some new and deeper disturbance in the air. It was fully a minute before she said simply:

'My father is dead.'

For an awkward moment or two he could think of nothing to say. Below, the steamer seemed abruptly to be cut in half, partially concealed by some promontory of rock on the shore, and then disappeared altogether.

'Would you have gone to the party if your father had been here?'

'Oh! that would have been quite different.' The tone of her words, not merely sad but aching, made him sense that his guess about the laughter had been right after all. 'But then if my father had been here there wouldn't have been any wedding.'

He said quietly that he didn't understand her. She laid the remaining half of her sandwich on the bench, clearly not wanting it, and simply sat with her glass in her hands.

'You saw Heinrich?' Yes, he remembered Heinrich, of the coarse stentorian brotherhood. 'One of the other men is his brother. Hermann. He is married to my elder sister.'

He sipped slowly at his wine, merely listening, and then was abruptly shocked to hear her say in a low voice entirely without vehemence but infinitely more startling than if she had yelled the words:

'They killed my father, the two of them.'

And then as if this statement were not brutal enough in itself she added, with the same devastating quietness:

'And yesterday I was all prepared to kill Heinrich.'

Her laughter and all his gay thoughts of Venice seemed suddenly an ashen mockery. He was gripped by two sudden fears: first that she was unbalanced, then that she was the victim of some monstrous delusion that would trap her, before she was aware of it, into some irretrievable ghastly folly.

'You shouldn't talk like that. I don't believe it anyway.'

'I don't care if you don't believe it. It happens to be true.'

In that moment he had half a mind to insist that she pulled herself together, stopped talking outrageous stupidities and went straight back to the party. But in his mind it all sounded like some fatuous piece of preaching and instead he put one arm round her, his hand on the cool bare rim of her upper shoulder.

At once he felt the gentle tension in himself build up again. Suddenly he wanted to kiss her but he knew it was no moment to kiss her and she startled him again by the most bewildering of statements:

'My mother and my sister are weak. My father had a vineyard – '

She went on to say that of course the vineyard was merely a sort of toy. It had nothing to do with the serious business of manufacturing soap and all that sort of thing. Her father had a vast enterprise. In the German way he worked like a ruthless demon to build and keep it up. He had about him young and energetic men like Hermann and Heinrich and he expected them to behave like ruthless demons too and, in time, under his guidance, they did. But the vineyard was always there too, a toy, a safety valve.

He was very fond of the vineyard. He liked to go there, especially in autumn, and climb up to the highest of the terraces and sit quietly shut away from the pressure of affairs and contemplate the grapes and the valley below. The grapes in that particular valley were allowed to hang on the vines until very late in the year, sometimes until almost December, and then were picked with infinite care, one by one.

He didn't care for driving cars very much and one early November day Hermann and Heinrich drove him in a big Mercedes up to the vineyard. It was a coldish day and the grapes were still hanging on the vines, golden-green, not yet ready for picking. Hermann at that time was already married to the elder sister and Heinrich had a shrewd and calculating eye on the younger.

'Have you ever gone around with the idea of killing somebody on your mind?'

'Good God, I should hope not.'

'It's a terrible, terrible thing.'

In a sudden fit of anguish she turned and impulsively pressed her face against him. Without a word he held her head in both hands, his lips pressed against her hair. Then in a second agonized moment she turned and pressed her mouth very close to his and begged him piteously not to let her do anything mad. Yesterday she almost had. Yesterday she'd driven a crazy, tormented hundred miles or more, utterly alone with the tortured notion that she might murder someone and then kill herself too.

Now did he see why she didn't want to go to the party? It was hardly a time for gay celebration. Up in the vineyard, that cold afternoon, her father had had a heart attack: not very desperate, at first, it seemed. He was conscious and begged the boys to drive him home.

'Instead Heinrich had the bright idea of driving ten miles to get a doctor. The calculating devil must have seen a kingdom falling into their laps. By the time they got back, nearly an hour later, he'd had a second attack. He died in the car, on the way home.'

Impulsively he kissed her on the lips.

It was more a gesture of comfort than anything else and she hardly seemed aware of it. When she spoke again it was as if she were finally attempting to purge herself of bitterness:

'I suppose it's really not Heinrich I hate most. It's my mother I can't forgive. She can see no wrong in them. They've got their kingdom now. They're the bosses. They've got what they wanted.'

She then kissed him of her own accord. She thanked him and said something about how she hadn't been able to talk to a single soul about all this and how it had been far easier to talk to a stranger, except that now he didn't seem so much like a stranger.

'You probably know me better than I know myself now.'

He folded her completely against him, putting his hand against one of her breasts. He was glad that she didn't push it away. He was glad too that she didn't start weeping, as he half-feared she would. All she said was:

'It's very nice being here with you.'

A moment later he saw the light on the sugar-cone go suddenly out. He contemplated the dark mountain for a few moments in silence and then said:

'Would you come to Venice tomorrow?'

'Oh! I couldn't.'

'Why not?'

'I have things to do.'

'What things?'

'Oh! many – all kinds – '

Suddenly he slipped his hand into the open neck of her dress, running his fingers across her bare breast.

'Please,' she said. 'You're hurrying things. I'd like a little time – '

'Now is the time.'

She became very quiet again. She seemed almost to go to sleep in his arms. Her head was low across his chest and he pressed his mouth against her hair. An unbelievable serenity flowered from all this and he lost completely all count of time until, drowsy himself, he roused up to hear somewhere down on the lakeside, a clock striking eleven.

'Are you awake?' he said. 'I wondered if the *Stube* might still be open. We could have a *Kirsch* – '

'That's a nice idea.'

They started to walk slowly down the hillside. He couldn't tell what her thoughts were now but she seemed, at last, immensely at peace with herself. And then, some way beyond the lowest of the waterfalls, he stopped and held her lightly by the shoulders and looked at her face.

'Come with me tomorrow.'

'I can't make up my mind.'

Jocularly he said why didn't they toss for it? He took a 10-*pfennig* piece from his pocket. Heads she would come with him, he joked, tails he would just take her away. Blithely he tossed the coin into the air, missed catching it again in the darkness and heard it go rolling and tinkling away down the road.

'Oh! God!' she suddenly said.

He had hardly time to wonder what this sudden nervous exclamation was about before he heard, from the foot of the slopes, a raucous chorus of men's voices and a tramp of marching feet.

'Heidi! Heidi! Heidi! Heidi! Heidi!' they were shouting, all in drilled stentorian unison, and it might have been that they were shouting '*Sieg Heil!*'

'Oh! God,' she said. 'I half expected something like this. Let's run for the *Stube* –'

They had hardly started running before he saw the ordered squad of penguins pounding up the slope, wild and wine-fired, some waving bottles, some in fancy hats, some skeined about with coloured streamers and all shouting the one brassy stentorian word:

'Heidi! Heidi! Heidi!'

Frightened now, she stopped and clutched him by the shoulders.

'Listen a moment. I will come tomorrow. I'll meet you here at seven – wait for me. I will come. But just at the moment – you won't be able to stop them – they've come to take me back –'

More like a pack of hunting dogs now the squad, suddenly catching sight of her, broke into disordered running, whooping and laughing. She gave him a single desperate kiss and then they were in for the kill, drunk and triumphant, yelling with evil idiocy, seizing her bodily and picking her up. In that moment all his own rage came seething back and he started shouting: 'God, you bastards! You bastards! You bastards!' flailing about with his fists. A second later a bottle hit him behind one ear. He dropped to his knees, half-stunned, and when he finally got to his feet again he knew it was no use any longer. They were already at the foot of the slope, running madly, carrying her away shoulder high, like someone on a bier.

In the morning, at seven o'clock, he walked slowly back up the slope. Some yards below the water-trough he caught sight of something glinting in the road and stooped and picked up the 10-*pfennig* piece he had dropped the night before.

'Heads you come with me. Tails I just take you away – '

He sat on the edge of the water-trough and waited, tossing the coin idly from one hand to another. There was a sharp chill in the air and once, when he dipped his hand into the water, he drew in his breath with shock. Gradually he heard the sound of all four quarters strike from the clock on the lakeside and then, soon after eight, he knew it was no use any longer.

He walked back to the hotel. The concierge, outside the vestibule, was taking an early morning breath of air.

'Have all the wedding guests gone?'

'Yes, sir. All of them. Every one.'

'What time did they leave?'

'Between five and six, sir. You mean you didn't hear them go, sir? They were very gay. They were very, very happy.'

He turned away. The first of the day's steamers was sliding swan-like across the lake and after watching it for a moment or two he turned and stared at the waterfalls, the lower meadows rich with flowers, the high mountains and a solitary woman hanging out clothes in a garden, between rows of red currant trees, shining crimson with ripening fruit.

But in reality he was neither watching nor listening to anything. All he could see were the eyes like palest blue campanulas; all he could hear was the echo of the voice of the girl with death in her heart.

Early One Morning

Mrs Daly, who had woken early in the warm summer morning, lay drowsily listening to what she thought was the sound of a thrush cracking a snail on the stone garden path outside.

Another day stretched before her like a long stale loaf. Ten hours of it would be cut off in dry, boring slices. At eight o'clock Mr Daly, umbrella neatly rolled, black homburg squarely set on his head, morning paper under his arm would be off to catch the London train; at six o'clock, umbrella neatly rolled, black homburg still squarely set, evening paper under his arm, he would be back again.

Mrs Daly listened to the thrush. Even thrushes, industriously cracking snails, had more excitement in their days than she did. Then slowly, as she listened, it struck her that there was something strange about the sound of the tapping thrush and soon she knew that she wasn't listening to a thrush at all.

What she could hear was the sound of feet running up and down.

With the beginnings of alarm she gave Mr Daly a sudden poke in the ribs and said:

'Stan, there's someone prowling about the garden. Listen. There's somebody outside.'

'Oh! Hell!' Mr Daly said.

'It's no use swearing about it like that. Get up and see who it is. You don't know who it might be. It's perhaps one of those soldiers from the depôt up to no good.'

'Oh! why in Heaven's name should soldiers – God, what time is it?'

'I don't know. The electric clock's gone to be repaired. What difference does the time make? Get up and see who it is. It might be someone breaking in.'

'Oh! Hell,' Mr Daly said.

Drowsy and fretful with temper, he swung his legs out of bed. Slowly his feet fumbled their way into his slippers. Even more slowly he tied the white cord of his pyjamas a little tighter.

'You hear such awful things nowadays,' Mrs Daly said. 'I'll get ready to telephone the police if it's anybody suspicious.'

'It's probably the postman with a registered letter – '

'It can't be. It's too early. I've been watching the sun come up.'

Mr Daly groped his way to the open bedroom window and stared mistily out. An unfriendly brightness, almost a glare, lay over everything, hurting his eyes. A thick dew covered the lawn and in the already strong sunlight the grass looked like a sheet of minutely shattered glass, each fragment glistening brilliantly.

'Ye gods and little fishes,' Mr Daly suddenly said, 'it's a stark raving lunatic!'

'Oh! no. Not one of them. Not from the St Saviour's mental – Oh! my goodness, I've heard they do get out sometimes – I'd better telephone – '

'He's stark, staring mad. He's running round the lawn with a ruddy great butterfly net.' Mr Daly craned his neck deeply out of the window and in an explosive voice shouted: 'Hey! you there – what the merry Hell are you doing in my garden? Get out of it! Go on – get out!'

An improbable figure of a man about forty, in grey slacks, pale green shirt and brown sandals performed a strange sort of spiralling act in the centre of the lawn, his large green butterfly net swivelling over his head, and then came to an abrupt and distressful halt, panting.

'Oh! pardon me. Excuse me. You haven't seen a budgerigar by any chance, have you? A blue one. It's my wife's. It flew over your garden fence just now – '

'Oh! tell it to the marines!' Mr Daly shouted and then

turned sarcastically to Mrs Daly, whispering, 'Says he's looking for his wife's budgerigar – '

'Well, perhaps he *is* – '

'Budgerigar or no budgerigar,' Mr Daly shouted, 'I damn well won't have you trampling all over my place! Get out of it!'

'I'm certain it's in here. I *know* it's in here. It's probably hiding among your roses – '

'Keep off my roses, damn you!'

'Don't get so worked up,' Mrs Daly said. 'If he has lost it why don't you go down and help him find it – '

'Me?' Mr Daly said, his voice bleakly choking. 'Me?'

'Yes,' Mrs Daly said, 'the poor little thing. It's probably terrified to death.'

'Let it be terrified!'

'It'll probably get caught by the cat or something. That would be horrible. All those precious blue feathers all over the lawn. Tell him you'll go down and help him.'

'I'll tell him no such thing,' Mr Daly said. 'Who the Beelzebub do you think I am? Go on – get out of it! Go and hunt your blasted budgerigar somewhere else! It's probably flown home to Mamma anyway by now. There, there, diddums lose ums Mamma then, sweetie precious? Did budgums think ums – '

'You really are rude,' Mrs Daly whispered. 'If you won't go down and help him I will.'

'Then you're a mug,' Mr Daly said. 'That's all I can say.'

'Don't call me a mug.'

'Every man's got a right to call his wife a mug if she turns out to be one.'

'I don't want that little bird killed in my garden,' Mrs Daly said. 'It would be on my conscience for ever.'

'Conscience,' Mr Daly said. 'Conscience? Hell, I'm going back to bed.'

As Mr Daly crawled like a growling dog under the bed-clothes Mrs Daly got out of bed and started to put on her dressing-gown, a petunia pink silk one, and her bedroom slippers, which were also pink and lined with pure white fur. With incredulous irritation Mr Daly stared at her over the edge of the sheet, telling her abruptly that she was mad.

'Well, that makes two of us,' she said. 'And anyway if you were anything of a man you'd go down and help and let me stay in bed.'

'Snap, snap!'

'Snap, snap! yourself. Perhaps one day you'll lose something and you'll be glad of someone to help you find it.'

'Lose what for instance?'

'Oh! anything.' Mrs Daly wrenched open the bedroom door with vigorous impatience. 'Me, for example. You never know.'

'Suffering cat-fish,' Mr Daly moaned, 'suffering cat-fish.'

Out in the garden the man in green shirt and grey slacks was gazing in dispirited fashion at the upper branches of a large laburnum tree, where the blue budgerigar was perching with unfluttering indifference in the morning sun.

'Winkie, Winkie!' he called and clapped his hands in gentle reprimand. 'Winkie – pay attention. Listen to me. You must come home. Do you hear? – you must come home to breakfast.'

At the conclusion of this sentence he turned to find Mrs Daly at his side. The unexpected sight of her in dressing-gown and nightdress quite unnerved him, so that he flushed slightly and said:

'Oh! I didn't mean to drag you out of bed. I really didn't –'

Something about these remarks seemed to strike him as being not quite right, so that he was embarrassed still further and tried to excuse himself by saying:

'You see the awful thing is that my wife will vow and declare I let him out. She did once before. He flew miles and miles away and we had the dickens of a job – I suppose you haven't a ladder by any chance, have you?'

'I think there must be one in the garage. Shall I get it?'

'Oh! no no. I'll go. I'll get it.'

'No, please. I'll go. You stay and watch the bird. Just in case he flies down.'

When Mrs Daly came struggling back with the ladder, a big wooden extendable one, the man was calling with piteous insistence into the laburnum tree:

'You must come home. Mumsie will be angry if you don't come. Mumsie will cry.'

Mrs Daly, staggering under the weight of the ladder, managed to gasp out:

'What does he usually have for breakfast? Perhaps if I fetched a few bread crumbs that might entice him – '

'Oh! he generally has corn-flakes with a little brown sugar. Oh! I'm so awfully sorry – let me have the ladder – Oh! by the way my name's Greenwood. I'm terribly sorry to inflict all this on you.'

While Mr Greenwood took over the struggle with the ladder Mrs Daly went into the house to fetch the brown sugar and the corn-flakes. With a rough clatter of wood on wood the ladder mounted the laburnum tree, first frightening the budgerigar so that it flew down and settled on a bush of cream roses and then bringing Mr Daly with renewed fury to the bedroom window.

'And what in hell are you doing with my ladder?' he shouted. 'Who in blazes do you think you are?'

'I'm trying to get up to the budgerigar – '

'Good God, man, it isn't there! It's on the far side of the garden. Sitting on a rose bush. I can see it from here.'

'Gracious me, so it is – '

In his sudden excitement Mr Greenwood let the ladder slip so that it crashed into the laburnum tree, splitting several branches. This event had barely started to madden Mr Daly afresh when he was utterly stunned to see his wife tripping across the dew-soaked lawn with a glass bowl of brown sugar in one hand and a packet of corn-flakes in the other.

Out of an astonished silence he managed at last to produce a wordless croak or two but these were too feeble for either Mrs Daly or Mr Greenwood to hear. By this time Mr Greenwood was approaching the bush of cream roses with the creeping stealth of a hunter of rare fauna. With coaxing whispers he begged the blue budgerigar to think of Mumsie and come home, at the same time waving his butterfly net. A few moments later the triumph of capture seemed to be almost within his grasp but at the crucial moment Mrs Daly called:

'Here I am with the sugar and the corn-flakes – '

The sudden sound of her voice startled the budgerigar into flight. With what seemed to be almost mischievous flutterings it crossed the rose-bed and flew over a thick cupressus hedge into the road beyond.

With the desperation of a man pursuing a runaway Mr Greenwood wrenched open the garden gate and gave chase, madly waving the butterfly net, with Mrs Daly only a yard or two behind him waving the corn-flakes and the bowl of sugar in excited unison.

Outside in the road a lost and bewildered Mr Greenwood stood staring this way and that, unable to see his pet, but joy flooded his face as Mrs Daly called:

'I see him! There he goes! Over there by the telephone box.'

Both Mr Greenwood and Mrs Daly started running. With a few last spasms of speechless wrath Mr Daly watched them go and then dragged himself back to bed, half-convinced he was part of some wakeful nightmare.

'He's perching on the top of the box,' Mrs Daly said. 'Perhaps if I put the corn-flakes and the sugar inside and held the door open he might be tempted to – '

'I rather fancy I could reach him with the net. But we'll have to be quiet. He's an awfully temperamental thing.'

While Mr Greenwood circled the telephone box with renewed stealth Mrs Daly put the bowl of sugar and the corn-flakes into the box and then stood outside, holding the door open. The air was breathless. The sudden clatter of a crate of milk bottles on the pavement farther down the road was merely one of the customary sounds of early morning and did nothing to disturb her at all.

She could now no longer see Mr Greenwood, who had gone into stealthy hiding on the far side of the box, and though she longed to know what was happening she had sense enough not to call. Once or twice she heard Mr Greenwood feeding the air with sweet whispers but otherwise a long time seemed to pass with nothing happening.

'Having a bit of late supper, lady? Or is it breakfast? Do you mind? I'd like to use the blower. My milk van's broken down.'

On the face of the early milkman there was an odd look of disbelief, irritation and sheer astonishment that was almost spiritual. As he gazed at Mrs Daly, her wet bedroom slippers and her nightdress protruding some six inches or so from under her dressing-gown, his lips seemed to be framing strange silent imprecations, as if in prayer.

'Oh! I'm so sorry. We're trying to catch a budgerigar.'

'We?'

The milkman, though accustomed to seeing incredible sights in the early morning, looked sharply round, rather as if expecting to see a crazy ghost.

A moment later one actually appeared in the form of Mr Greenwood, madly running.

'He's gone again! You frightened him off! There he goes!'

With lean strides Mr Greenwood tore off down the road, waving the butterfly net. Mrs Daly snatched up the bowl of sugar and the packet of corn-flakes and followed in enthusiastic pursuit, to be watched with a sort of drugged patience by the milkman, who finally called out with some acidity that they should try putting salt on its tail.

Three hundred yards down the road a heavily panting Mr Greenwood came to a halt under the last street lamp, on the arm of which the budgerigar was perched with the sly calm that both precedes and succeeds mischief. With little breath left Mr Greenwood could only shake a trembling forefinger in admonishment, his eyes actually watering with fatigue.

Presently Mrs Daly arrived, panting too. A certain archness, almost a smooth scorn, was now evident in the pose of the budgerigar, whose flight had left it both fresh and exhilarated.

'I've just thought of something,' Mrs Daly said. 'Doesn't he have a mate? Don't these birds pine if they don't have company? I mean they're love-birds, aren't they?'

'No, he doesn't,' Mr Greenwood said. 'We're always meaning to get another, but somehow – Winkie, do come down now. Do be a good boy and come down.'

'Yes, Wee Willie Winkie,' Mrs Daly said, 'you're really very naughty. Why didn't you stay in your nice cage? You'll get eaten by a cat.'

'Oh! dear, don't say that. That would be the last straw. My wife would go mad.'

'Did you notice how sharply he looked at me when I called him Wee Willie?' Mrs Daly said. 'He looked quite shaken. I believe he *knows* – I mean I think he's aware of me as a person. Do you know what? I somehow believe he'd let me catch him. Give me the net.'

'It's far too high. You'd never reach.'

Mrs Daly set the packet of corn-flakes and the bowl of sugar on the pavement and then suddenly kicked off her bedroom slippers.

'I could if you'd let me stand on your back. That would give me another yard. I'm not heavy.'

'Oh! Lord, I don't know –'

'It's either that or the cat,' Mrs Daly said. 'After all we're nearly out to the woods here. Once he gets into the woods we'll never catch him.'

'All right, then. Just one try. I feel awful at having dragged you all the way out here.'

'Not half as awful as you'd feel if you went home without him. Now Wee Willie Winkie, listen.' Mrs Daly addressed Wee Willie Winkie in the sternest possible terms. 'I'm coming to get you. And get you I will. I'll stand no nonsense from you, you little blue devil. Do you hear?'

The budgerigar, looking down at Mr Greenwood already bending his back, actually seemed to hear.

'You'll have to bend a little lower,' Mrs Daly said. 'I can't quite reach.'

Mr Greenwood crouched lower on his haunches.

'Have you got the net?' he said. 'The thing to try and do is not swipe at him.'

Mrs Daly said yes, she had the net and she'd try not to swipe. A moment later she climbed on Mr Greenwood's back, clutching the butterfly net in one hand and holding the lamp-post with the other. Then Mr Greenwood raised himself gently upward by something like another foot, at the same time clutching the lamp-post with both hands for support. He had never had a woman standing on his back before and the experience suddenly reminded him sharply of a game called mop-stick which he had often played as a boy.

'Gently does it,' he said. 'Gently.'

There was no word of response from Mrs Daly but suddenly Mr Greenwood was convinced that he heard footsteps.

'Just making the tea?'

The voice of the policeman returning from night duty was inquisitive and gentle. With calm appraisal he stared at Mrs Daly's bare feet, her cast-off bedroom slippers, the fringe of her nightdress, the butterfly net, the corn-flakes, the bowl of sugar and the bent back of Mr Greenwood, who was unable to see the policeman except through his legs.

'Oh! Lord – no, we're trying to catch a budgerigar – '

'No, Wee Willie Winkie, don't you dare move!'

'So it's Wee Willie Winkie, is it?' the policeman said.

'And I suppose he's running through the town in his night-gown too?'

'I've nearly got him,' Mrs Daly said. 'I'll have him in a moment now – Oh! blast! You wicked little wretch! He's flown.'

In sudden vexation Mrs Daly sat down on Mr Green-wood's back, then promptly slid off it, showing several inches of her bare knees. Again with calm appraisal the policeman stared at her as if all this was, as with the milkman, an everyday affair.

'Excuse me, madam, but have you been to bed or are you just going? Or what?'

'Oh! I've been. I've been up hours.'

'And does your husband here usually let you wander about the streets in your nightdress, madam?'

'Oh! he's not my husband.'

'Oh! he's not? It's like that, is it? I see.'

'Oh! it's not like that,' Mr Greenwood said. 'It's not at all like that. Not at all.'

'Then what is it like sir?' With light scepticism, the policeman stared at the packet of corn-flakes and the bowl of sugar. 'Just going to have breakfast, too, I take it?'

'Oh! no. The idea of the corn-flakes and the sugar is to catch the budgerigar.'

'I see. And does he have cream with them too?'

'He doesn't like cream.'

The policeman gave a sudden long deep sigh, as if for a moment seriously questioning his own sanity. In the en-suing silence Mrs Daly put on her bedroom slippers, at the same time smiling at the policeman, who failed to smile back and merely put his head to one side.

Then after remarking that it was a matter of great interest to hear that the budgerigar didn't like cream the police-man invited Mr Greenwood with no great urgency but rather with an almost sublime patience to present him with some sort of explanation as to what exactly was going on.

'Oh! it's quite simple,' Mrs Daly said. 'I woke up early and thought I heard a thrush cracking a snail on the garden path but it wasn't.'

'Oh! you did? Go on.'

'Then I knew it was footsteps. I was worried because I thought it might be an escaped lunatic from St Saviour's and then my husband looked out of the window and saw this gentleman in the garden. With this butterfly net.'

The policeman surveyed Mr Greenwood with an air of keenest inquiry.

'So that's where you're from, is it?'

'Oh! no, no,' Mr Greenwood said. 'Not at all. Not at all. That's a great mistake. I'm not from there at all.'

'How do I know?' With icy alacrity the policeman turned to Mrs Daly and her butterfly net. 'How do I know you're not both from there?'

'Don't be insulting.'

With dignified hands the policeman unbuttoned the breast pocket of his tunic and took out his pencil and notebook.

'Madam, I'm afraid I shall have to ask you for your name.'

'And supposing I refuse to give it?'

'That would be very foolish – that's if you're asking my opinion.'

'I wouldn't dream of asking your wretched opinion. I've just given you a perfectly rational explanation of what Mr Greenwood and I are doing here and you haven't the grace or sense to accept it.'

'Madam – '

Suddenly Mr Greenwood let out lyrical cries of delight.

'He's back! He's at the corn-flakes! He must be hungry.'

With outstretched hands Mr Greenwood darted to the corn-flake box, on which the budgerigar was now perching with an air at once innocent and bold. In a matter of seconds the capture was over. Deftly Mr Greenwood slipped the budgerigar into his trousers' pocket like some unwanted glove and then made a gesture of elation, almost as if to put his arm round Mrs Daly.

'Oh! Mrs Daly, you've been wonderful. You've been absolutely marvellous. You really have. I don't know how to thank you.'

'So it's Mrs Daly, is it?'

As in a dream the policeman sketched at the air with his pencil.

'Yes, I'm Mrs Daly.'

'And it's Mr Greenwood, is it?'

'Yes.'

The policeman drew a gargantuan breath as if preparatory to some sort of explosion and then let air slowly expire.

'All right, Mrs Daly and Mr Greenwood, I'll give you exactly thirty seconds to make yourselves scarce. And when I say scarce I mean scarcer than that! Corn-flakes an' all! – '

All the way home Mr Greenwood repeated over and over again how wonderful Mrs Daly had been, how grateful he was for the brilliant idea of the corn-flakes and with what a different outlook he could now face the day. In turn she said she'd done it for the bird's sake. She hated the thought of suffering in animals and birds. She simply hadn't been able to bear the thought of those dead blue feathers on the lawn. It had all been so exciting.

'It's wonderful to start a day doing something like this,' she said. 'It makes you feel – Oh! I don't know. Almost like a bird – '

In this sustained mood of elation she almost tripped into the kitchen, to find Mr Daly wreathed in bluish smoke and scraping with a table knife at a square of scorched toast. Gaily she said something about being back at last and Mr Daly regarded her with a cold, sour eye.

'Back from where? A trip to Mars? You've been gone hours.'

'If I've been gone twenty minutes it's as much as it is.'

'Hours and hours I tell you. And what about my breakfast?'

'What about it? It surely wouldn't have broken your back to cook yourself a couple of slices of bacon?'

With grim disbelief Mr Daly stared down at her dew-soaked bedroom slippers.

'Your feet are soaked. Where the hell have you been? Have you been rampaging about the streets like that?'

'I have not been rampaging anywhere. I've been helping to rescue a bird from being mauled by a cat.'

'God help me.'

'Perhaps He would if you'd put yourself in other people's shoes occasionally.'

'I do not want to put myself in other people's shoes!' Mr Daly said. 'It's quite bad enough being in my own.'

'There's no need to shout even if it is.'

'I'm not shouting.'

'It's like Bedlam.'

'It damn well *is* Bedlam. It's ruddy lunacy. What will people think? My wife rampaging the streets with a strange man at the crack of dawn, chasing a stupid budgerigar. I wonder you didn't get run in.'

'As a matter of fact I very nearly did.'

Mrs Daly actually laughed at the memory of the police-man, but Mr Daly merely choked sharply and threw the piece of burnt toast into the sink.

'God Almighty, what were you thinking of? Whatever possessed you?'

'Nothing possessed me. I was simply doing what I thought was right.'

'Right!' Mr Daly said. 'Right! Ye gods, right!'

'I'm going upstairs to change my slippers now,' Mrs Daly said. 'I'll be back directly to cook your breakfast. By the way, could you lend me five pounds until tomorrow?'

'What in hell for?'

'To buy something, naturally.'

'To buy what?'

'I don't think you'd understand.'

'Even money-lenders might at least be given the chance of understanding.'

'Oh! very well,' Mrs Daly said, 'if you must know it's to buy a budgerigar.'

'A *what*? Don't tell me you're going to start keeping those damn things now?'

'No, I'm not. As a matter of fact it's going to be a companion for the other budgerigar.'

'I'm mad,' Mr Daly said, actually grasping the kitchen table to support himself. 'I'm clean crackers – '

'They pine,' Mrs Daly said. 'When they're alone, I mean. That's why they're called love-birds.'

'Don't tell me. Don't tell me.'

'It's rather strange when you come to think of it, isn't it, that a bird can pine for love? Just like a human being.'

'Why like a human being? Why can't they just be themselves?'

Mrs Daly left the kitchen without providing an answer. Mr Daly sat down heavily at the kitchen table and stared hard at the front page of the morning paper. Everything was worse than awful. If he didn't get breakfast soon he'd miss the morning train. Even if he didn't miss it he wouldn't get a decent seat. He'd have to sit with a lot of bounders he didn't know. They'd try to strike up conversations on politics or football or the Common Market or something and he'd never be able to do the cross-word, which he reckoned to finish every morning in thirty-six minutes flat. If that happened anything could happen. Once you got a day started like that it was hell.

'One egg or two?'

Mrs Daly, wearing red slippers now, tripped into the kitchen in a still higher mood of elation, half-singing, half-laughing.

'What on earth you can find to sing and laugh about God only knows,' Mr Daly said. 'I'm blessed if I can. It's going to be one of those days. I can feel it. It's going to be ruddy awful.'

Mrs Daly, laughing again, broke an egg into a cup. Already it seemed to her that half the day had evaporated like a dream.

'You think so?' she said. 'I think it's going to be an absolutely marvellous day. I'm perfectly, perfectly happy.'

Squiff

HE had always been a drifter. He moved from place to place as the fancy took him, working mostly as a kitchen porter or cellarman or handyman in hotels, along the coast in summertime and then back inland for winter.

He was a trustworthy, stocky little man, not exactly stunted but perhaps what some people would have called a runt: rather simple-looking in a taciturn sort of way but with what were normally good, capable, steady hands. He hardly ever drank and was one of the few of his kind who did no gambling: probably because he had never learned to read or write, so that he could never be quite sure what the names of the horses were.

Somehow or other he had picked up his odd nick-name: Squiff. Nothing could have suited him less. Instead it seemed to mock him. It seemed really to belong to someone else, to a jocular sprightly man with a beery squint in his eye who took life gaily and made easy friends. He on the other hand never made many friends, nor enemies for that matter, and he was hardly ever jocular.

When he was a little over forty he got himself a job as handyman at a country hotel called *The Montague Arms*. It was a big fake-baronial style house heavily panelled in oak and decorated with gleaming battle-axes, suits of armour, coats-of-arms and portraits in oils of obscure Tudor gentlemen. The large chilly rooms lacked intimacy. Most of the guests found themselves talking in half-whispers and when anyone raised a voice the effect seemed aggressive, even coarse. Perhaps because of this, or perhaps because the food itself was merely indifferent, not a lot of people came to eat there. As a consequence the staff were bored and restless and, like Squiff, always drifting on.

Soon after he got there, on a warm Saturday night in July,

it happened that the hotel wine-waiter was careless enough to slip on the stone flagstones of a passage while carrying a tray of glasses. In falling he put out an arm, jabbed it flat on a broken glass and severed an artery.

Probably because the night was so exceptionally warm and fine there were an unusual number of guests in the dining-room. One of the waitresses was sick at the sight of blood and sat outside for the rest of the evening, trembling in a chair, and there was no one to serve wine at the tables until suddenly someone remembered Squiff. The suit of tails they put on him was a little on the large side and the wing collar, over-large too, merely heightened his look of simplicity. He looked altogether clumsy, lost and un-dignified.

As soon as he went into the dining-room a rending shout of 'Waiter!' hit him like a growl from a raging boar. When he answered it he found himself facing a broad, heavy-faced man named Lubbock who was dining at a corner table with a blonde-haired girl of remarkably cool and distinguished appearance, in a low-cut dress of silver blue, who seemed altogether out of place in the company of a second-hand car dealer notorious for loudness of mouth, brutish habits and too much money.

'Where's the bloody *Liebfraumilch* I ordered twenty minutes ago?' Lubbock shouted. His lips, coarse as the crêpe soles of a shoe, champed out the words viciously enough to make Squiff recoil. 'And anyway where's the wine-waiter? You're not the bloody wine-waiter, are you?'

'Yessir. I am now.'

'What do you mean you am now?'

Squiff, who always talked with a good deal of hesitation, started to explain about the accident but Lubbock, furiously stubbing out one cigarette and in another second lighting another, shouted that he didn't want to hear a lot of crap like that. He wanted the wine – and bloody fast too.

All this time the girl was watching Squiff. Her thick fair hair fell over her bare shoulders like a mane. Her very light blue eyes were as cool and fresh as spring water and the way she looked at him was full of stillness.

He went away, pondered for a few minutes, decided he hadn't a notion which wine had been ordered and then went back into the dining-room with the wine-list. Would the gentleman mind telling him again which wine he wanted?

'The *Liebfraumilch*, you flapping wet! How many more times? I have it every time I come here. They keep it specially for me.'

'Perhaps you wouldn't mind just pointing it out on the list for me, sir?'

'It isn't on the bloody list, you damn fool. I tell you they keep it specially for me. Are you going to bring the damn stuff or do I have to fetch it myself?'

'I'm bringing it, sir.'

Again, all this time, the girl sat watching him, never moving an eyelid. Again her eyes had that great penetrative stillness in them. She seemed to be looking completely through him and it was almost as if she had already discovered what his great trouble was: the fact that he couldn't read or write and that therefore, for him, the names of wines, like those of horses, were for ever locked in mystery.

He finally got over the trouble with the help of the barman, who also gave him some brief advice. 'Better ask which number on the list people want, Squiff. The bins are all numbered in the cellar and I'll show you which is which.'

Several minutes later he was on his way back to the dining-room with the bottle of *Liebfraumilch* when, half-way down the broad baronial corridor, he found himself face to face with the girl. It didn't strike him for a long time afterwards that she might have intentionally made an excuse to come out there simply for the purpose of helping him. He could only stand there, at that moment, looking as stiff and vacuous as one of the faceless suits of armour stuck up against the wall.

'Did you manage to find it?' she said.

'Think so, miss. Is this the one?'

'That's the one.' She laid her hand on the bottle and the way he felt himself start suddenly she might have been laying it on his arm. 'Yes, the temperature's about right. You'd better get another one up too. Mr Lubbock's sure to want another.'

She smiled and for what seemed to be about half a minute he stood utterly transfixed. He had nothing at all to say; but already the greatest of all possible wonders had started to grow in his mind: how it could come about that a girl of her sort, clothed with that beautiful, well-mannered stillness, could have mixed herself up with a man like Lubbock? It was all completely beyond him.

'And don't forget that Mr Lubbock likes me to taste the wine first. He says my palate's good. You'll remember that, won't you?'

'Yes, miss.'

She smiled and then, for the first time, his hands started trembling. They were to suffer these bouts of acute trembling for several months afterwards. Sometimes they lasted for only a minute or so, sometimes for half an hour, but that first evening he was still shaking when he started to pour the wine at Lubbock's table.

As the first drops went into the girl's glass Lubbock gave a pugnacious sort of growl.

'How the hell did you know Miss Howard liked to taste the wine?'

'Ladies first, sir.'

'You'll do.' Lubbock gave a half-belch that might almost have been a note of praise. 'I shall want another bottle of this, do you hear?'

'Yessir. Ready whenever you want it.'

'It'd better be. And watch what you're up to. You're all of a bloody shake.'

The girl had been watching his trembling hands and now she looked straight up at him. Immediately something in the very fullness of the stare calmed him down completely. And then as if she wanted to put him finally at rest she said: 'Your face seems familiar. Didn't you used to work at *The Dolphin* at Brighton?'

'No, miss. Never worked there.'

'Funny. I seem to have seen you somewhere before.'

'Don't think so, miss.'

'Ah! well, we shall be seeing you again I expect.'

'Expect so, miss.'

He was about to move away when Lubbock growled 'What's your name, anyway? What do they call you?'

'Squiff.'

'By God, you look it.' Lubbock gave a short crackling laugh that was more like an amused snarl. 'Hear that, Stella? Squiff. How's that for a name?'

Lubbock laughed a second time but by the time the sound had echoed round the high-pitched dining-room Squiff had gone.

He had hardly left the table before Lubbock drained his glass and then, sloshing more wine into it, gave another insolent boar-like growl from the lips that were so like lumps of crêpe rubber, telling the entire dining-room:

'This place gets worse and worse. It's going down the bloody drain. You can tell that. It'd better pick up or I'll be hanged if we come here.'

'I like it here.'

'All right, if you like it that's all right then. If it's good enough for you – '

She accepted this rough compliment as if it were a gem. An extraordinary look of entrancement, almost adoration, came over her face, precisely as if she could see behind the brutish crêpe-like lips some engaging quality in Lubbock that was lost on the rest of the world.

'Just like you to say that,' she said. 'Having a nice time?'

'All right. You?'

'Lovely. The wine's just right on an evening like this. Somehow it never tastes the same anywhere else as it does here.'

What exactly prompted Squiff to begin to send her flowers every week was something he could probably have never been able to explain. It might have been the only way he knew of saying thank you for the help she had given him; it was something he couldn't possibly have expressed in words. It might equally have been that he was trying to express, in silence and from far off, an otherwise inexpressible adoration.

It might also have been something of both these things but it wasn't long before he heard that she was living with Lubbock in a farmhouse seven or eight miles away and there, every Saturday morning, bunches of red roses arrived, always without a card.

Lubbock had called her Miss Howard, but in reality she was still married to a man of Quaker sympathies named Bailey who kept a small stationery and fancy goods shop of an old fashioned sort in the nearest market town. Bailey was the sort of man who, rather than draw ten cheques to pay ten bills, would draw one cheque and walk round the town paying each bill by cash, thus saving nine cheque stamps. When he bought her a new coat or dress – and it hadn't been very often – he gave her cash too and then insisted on having the few shillings, or even few pennies, change. It didn't need much coaxing on Lubbock's part to make her see that life could offer more than this kind of parsimony. She stepped in a few months from ready-made coats and chain store dresses to mink wraps, hats from Mayfair, a car of her own and frequent trips across to the French coast to gamble and drink champagne on Sundays.

'A girl like you's got to see the sights,' Lubbock said.

There are certain women who, though having refinements of their own, appear to relish a quality of brashness in a man. Lubbock loved her harshly, rudely and even brutally and in a strange way it excited her. The greatest of her qualities was not that she was very good looking but that she was gifted with curious powers of penetration. She saw behind all the barking insolence of Lubbock's exterior a man desperately aware of his own deficiencies; the outer animal concealed a baby groping.

In the same way she had been able to detect, or at least guess at, the deficiencies in Squiff. She was quick to sense something more than a nervous upheaval of incompetence behind the trembling hands.

But when the roses began to arrive she failed to put the fact of them and Squiff together; it never once crossed her mind that the two might have a connexion. At first she felt inclined to treat them as a joke but after two or three weeks they started to affect her in quite another way. She felt herself making something intensely secretive of them and when Lubbock teased her about them in his coarsest fashion she merely lied in rather a clumsy way.

'New boy friend turned up trumps again, I see. More roses, eh? Generous bastard – a whole bleeding dozen again. Have to watch himself or he'll be broke soon.'

'I have them sent myself,' she said. 'They're the new Baccarat roses. A special sort. I like them because they last so long.'

All the time, still acting as wine-waiter up at the hotel, Squiff waited for one Saturday after another. He hoped always that she would wear one of the roses in her dress at dinner but she never did. This hope threw him into a tremendous battle to keep himself calm but he could never manage to control the shaking of his hands.

One evening, as the weather turned sharply chilly in late September, Lubbock decided to drink red wine instead of white at dinner.

'We'll have number 15,' he said, 'the *Nuits St George*' – he pronounced it *Newts Saint George* and in a strange way something inside Stella Howard wept for him – 'and see it's the right bloody temperature. Nice and warm. I don't want my guts froze out tonight.'

Squiff fetched up two bottles of wine from the cellar, found a convenient radiator, put the bottles on top and waited for them to warm up.

Ten minutes later Stella Howard was doing her best not to pretend that she knew the wine was cooked. Squiff's hands, as usual, were shaking violently and something about them and about the way she stared up at him as he started to pour a quivering trickle of wine aroused in Lubbock a violent rush of suspicions.

'Tip some in here!' he ordered. 'I'll taste it.'

He drank rapidly at the wine and immediately jumped as if scalded.

'You flaming wet! It's like hot soup! Take the bloody stuff away.'

Squiff stood helpless, without a word, his hands still violently shaking. Stella Howard stared up at him in uneasy pity, without a word either. The clatter of a spoon falling on the bare oak floor at the far end of the dining-room was like a sudden signal to Lubbock, who abruptly turned on her in a lash of rage, for once not loud, but curt and cold.

'And what are you grinning at? You harboured him in it, didn't you? You knew it was cooked, didn't you?'

'I am not grinning.'

'You were grinning like a bloody heifer.'

She at once took the mink wrap from the back of her chair, slipped it over her shoulders and got up.

'And where d'ye think you're going?' he said.

She merely stared coldly past him, closed the wrap firmly across the front of her dress and started to walk away. She had hardly moved from the table before Lubbock leapt up, took one long stride towards her and half-pushed, half-knocked her back in the chair.

'Don't make a damn fool of yourself. Sit down.'

She sat there without attempting to make another move. There were tears in her eyes. The wrap, falling slowly from her bare shoulders, slid to the floor.

For a few miraculous moments Squiff's hands had stopped trembling and he stooped down to pick up the wrap. He had hardly moved before Lubbock said:

'And what are you dancing about at? She doesn't want

any help from you. When she wants any help from you she'll send you a wire.'

Without answering or looking at either Lubbock or the girl Squiff walked away. He had seen the gleam of tears in her eyes and he carried the image away with him. As the evening went on the image grafted itself painfully and permanently on to his own eyes, so that not only was he afflicted with new, greater shakings of his hands but his vision was clouded too.

'I'll kill him,' he started telling himself. 'I'll kill him. I'm going to kill him. Somehow.'

All the next week the idea of killing Lubbock chattered through his mind like a tortuous and clumsy tune. It drove him about in a daze. It kept him awake for fearful stretches in the night, his mind cold and haunted and indecisive. In his customary groping and innocent way he tried to fix on some method of killing Lubbock and finally came to a grotesquely childish conclusion.

'Got to look like an accident,' he kept telling himself. 'Got to look like an accident somehow.'

What sort of accident it was going to be he couldn't, for a long time, make up his mind. There was nothing in his nature remotely subtle enough to make any kind of ingenious plan. He merely groped; and in groping got himself into darker confusions where the only things of any abiding clarity were the tears in Stella Howard's eyes, the way her wrap had slid to the floor and the way she had first looked at him. All the time he thought of the great stillness in her eyes.

By the following Saturday night, still without any real idea of what sort of accident it was to be, his nerves were screwed up like wire rope. His hands trembled constantly. His order for roses had gone off as usual and now and then he was able to pacify himself for a moment by dwelling on another secret image: that of Stella Howard unpacking the roses, putting them in a vase, gazing at them and perhaps for a few moments wondering who had sent them. He would never be able to know what her feelings about the roses were but it calmed him briefly to think of it.

Then an unexpected thing happened. Just before half-past seven the head waiter came up to him and said:

'Mr Lubbock's just cancelled his table. Says he won't be in tonight.'

He immediately felt desolate and lonely. The urge to kill Lubbock suddenly receded. The mere fact that he wasn't going to see Stella Howard, even as a figure in a painful scene, put him in a new and different sort of daze. It was exactly as if they had been married or lovers and she had left him. It was almost as if she, and not Lubbock, had died.

He spent the whole of the following week battered by these opposing ideas: on the one hand of wanting to kill Lubbock and on the other of wanting to see Stella Howard back, as it were, from the dead. The nagging aridity of his thoughts was so great that for the first time in his life he started to take a few drinks. On evenings when the hotel was half-empty he stayed for long periods down in the cellar, staring into the half darkness with a glass in his hands.

Drink didn't help him much; it merely seemed to push the days along a fraction faster towards another Saturday.

And when Saturday came he had another surprise. He was walking through the bar about half past six when he suddenly heard Lubbock's voice, for some reason not so loud as usual, and saw him sitting at the bar. The night was cold and squally and Lubbock's voice sounded curiously brittle, very like an echo of the many pine boughs cracking in the rough wind outside:

'Ah! it's old Squiff. How's our old Squiff?' Lubbock lugubriously waved a glass of gin about and wagged a heavy cautionary finger. 'Look a bit pale and drawn, Squiff, old sport. Should take more of this – more of the old oil, eh?'

'Evening, sir.'

'More of the old oil, that's what keeps the bloody cold out, eh?'

Squiff didn't want to talk; he started to leave the bar.

'Here, half a mo, where are you off to? Come 'ere a minute.'

Squiff, wondering over and over again where Stella Howard could be, stood motionless by the door. Behind Lubbock's back the barman was making a prolonged pretence of polishing a bar that was in no need of polishing and Squiff said in a steady voice, his hands surprisingly steady too:

'I was just off down the cellar, sir. Thought I might get your usual up. You'll have the red, I suppose?'

'Not eating tonight, Squiff. No bleeding appetite.'

Squiff, staring straight at Lubbock, felt his whole body tautening up, stiffening with a fresh, sharp hatred of the man.

'Madam not coming in tonight, sir?'

'Blast madam. To bloody hell with madam –'

Out of the turbulent stream of alcoholic mutterings – drink seemed to twist the character of Lubbock inside out, suppressing both insolence and the louder of his coarsenesses, turning him introspective – it gradually grew clear that he and Stella Howard had been quarrelling long and bitterly that afternoon. There wasn't much that was coherent in Lubbock's muttered repetitions until Squiff, in a moment of paralytic astonishment, heard the words, repeated several times:

'Red roses. The sod sends her red roses, regular as bloody clockwork. Every damn week – there they are, stuck all over the blasted place. Nothing but red roses –'

Squiff's hands started shaking; the sinews jumped as if from acute bursts of electric shock. His tongue recoiled and pressed itself like a short snake against the back of his mouth and he heard Lubbock say:

'They're all bitches, the whole stinking lot of 'em. You give 'em the bloody world and they take it and then throw it back into your wet physog. Bitches – they stink, the whole lot of 'em – they're only good for one thing –'

Squiff, not waiting to hear any more, turned suddenly, walked out of the bar and then out of the hotel. It was dark

early that night and nips of rain were falling in the squalls.
Pine boughs were cracking off like so many fireworks. He
stood for some moments under the pines, shaking dreadfully,
not really consciously thinking, not stopping to ask himself
whether in fact Lubbock knew who had sent the flowers or
whether it mattered if he did.

There was only one thing in his mind. The shape the
accident was to take had suddenly become perfectly clear to
him. It was all of miraculous simplicity.

Instinctively he looked round for Lubbock's car and saw
it, a big black Mercedes, parked under a big chestnut tree
at the upper end of the hotel drive. So early in the evening
there were no other cars about and without a second's
hesitation he walked over to it, his hands still shaking in that
dreadfully helpless fashion, his mind and ears not really conscious, so that he wasn't even aware of the odd chestnut or
two that sudden squalls ripped out of the tree and sent
bumping down on the asphalt below.

In another minute or two he had found a wheel-brace and
a screw-driver in the boot of the car. It was all of a miraculous, grotesque simplicity. Presently he had taken off
one of the front wheel hub-covers and was loosening the
wheel-nuts with the brace. The concentrated pressure necessary to turn the nuts had the effect of locking his hands
to the brace, so that for some time they actually stopped
shaking.

With the loosening of each nut he seemed to see Lubbock,
drunk, careering helplessly down some distant hill in the
squally darkness, the front wheel of the Mercedes flying off.
The thing was of such fabulous simplicity that no one, he
told himself, would ever know. But just to make doubly
sure, he thought, he would loosen a second wheel.

He had actually started unscrewing the first nut of the
front on-side wheel when a big taxi came up the drive in the
rain. In a vague way he was aware of it stopping, of hearing
one of its doors slam and of a couple of voices talking. But it
didn't occur to him to hide himself. He was thirty or more

yards away and most of the sounds were muffled in the squalls.

Presently the taxi turned and drove off, head-lights swinging under the pines. For a few minutes he worked on at the remaining nuts, hands still not shaking, with the vision of Lubbock in a death-spin still vibrantly clear in his mind.

It took him fully another minute to realize that someone was standing by his side, watching him. He slowly looked up. It was Stella Howard standing there; she was wearing a bright yellow mackintosh and a blue scarf on her head.

'What are you doing to Mr Lubbock's car?'

Her voice was a low whisper but the loudest of shouts couldn't have hit him with greater shock. His hands were suddenly taken by a gigantic spasm of trembling. It was exactly as if another pair of hands, invisible and frenziedly muscular, had violently seized hold of them and given them a shaking of superhuman power.

He was helpless to stop this shaking and he didn't say a word. For almost another minute she didn't speak either but all the time she was looking at him in that same steadfast way, her eyes full of a miraculous stillness, as when she had first sensed the greatest of his troubles, the fact that he couldn't read or write.

Now for the second time she understood what he was doing. It was all perfectly clear to her and she was very calm.

'That would be a terrible thing to do.'

Again he didn't say a word and she stood looking down with pity at that dreadful trembling of his hands. She might have been moved to say, in that moment, something about the roses, how she knew who had sent them and why, or to chastise him or in some way threaten him for the thing he was about to do.

But she didn't speak either. Instead she suddenly took hold of his hands and gripped them with her own. She held them like that for fully five minutes, neither she nor Squiff speaking, the squally rain flicking hard at their two silent faces, until the shaking of his hands stopped at last and he was completely quiet again.

Then she said, still very calm: 'Promise you'll never do anything like that again. There's no way out of a thing like that. It would be an awful thing to have blood on your – '

She broke off. He stood mute in the rain. The slight twist of his head was more like a flicker of terror than any acknowledgement of what she had said and the quick sucking in of his lips, almost child-like, was the only sound he made.

She had nothing else to say to him but suddenly, at the last moment, she bent down, hesitated and then quickly kissed him on the back of both hands. Then she turned sharply and went into the hotel to find Lubbock and in another moment Squiff took the wheel-brace and started winding up the nuts, head tucked down on his chest in the driving rain.

Nowadays he no longer works in hotels. He sells evening newspapers, inland in winter and along the coast in summertime. Sometimes in the invigorating summer air he actually runs along the sea-shore, crying the racing results, the scandals, the catastrophes, the world scares and the latest murders as they happen. And sometimes, prompted by some juicier piece of news, he is actually jocular.

And just occasionally, but only occasionally, his hands start shaking briefly again. But on the whole, especially when he thinks of Stella Howard, he keeps them steady as a rock.

The Primrose Place

SHE was gathering the last of the cooking apples on the high slope of the orchard when she suddenly turned her head and saw him groping his way up the narrow lane. Like a man in the advanced stages of drunkenness he was lurching irregularly from side to side between the high banks, occasionally stopping for a few unsteady seconds to peer into the hedgerows, almost as if expecting even in late October to find a bird's nest there.

She was so convinced that he was drunk that when he finally stopped by the orchard gate and flung one arm flatly out on the top rail of it and stared with mild sightlessness through the trees she instinctively lowered herself a step or two down the ladder and crouched behind the apple trunk. Her basket was hanging by a steel hook from a branch just level with her head and she set it clumsily swaying by a knock from her elbow. When she steadied it by holding the hook tight in her hand the slightly cold touch of steel on her palm made her realize for the first time how frightened she was. She instinctively gripped the hook more tightly and told herself:

'If he comes for me I shall use it. It's all I've got.'

Then suddenly she heard him give something between a retch and groan, followed by what might have been the word 'God', repeated several times. All this time she was afraid to look at him and could only think, foolishly rather than desperately:

'I've got my dungarees on. I've got my dungarees on. That'll make it more difficult. And the hook. I've got the hook.'

Then when she looked at him again she realized that he was utterly unaware of her being there. He wasn't even looking in her direction. His arms were drawn together now, the

66

hands close together under his chin, tightly gripping a black wooden box about nine inches square. The box appeared in some way to be of desperate importance to him. Once he actually seemed to be about to press his mouth against it but instead he jerked his head sharply upwards and stared with almost fanatically wide blue eyes at the sky.

It was the intense blueness of the eyes that suddenly made her realize that her first impressions of him were entirely wrong. She knew now that he was neither drunk nor, as she had first imagined, middle-aged. He was quite young, per-haps twenty-eight or so, not much younger than herself, she thought. And something about the wide directionless stare of the eyes gave him not merely a great air of weariness. It might also have been that, for some crazy reason, his memory had gone.

For the next half minute or so the temperature of her fear dropped a little. She no longer gripped the steel hook so tightly. Then suddenly a big apple, falling from one of the topmost branches of the tree, bounced from bough to bough and finally hit the ground with a thud that seemed to bring him, for about half a minute, to his senses.

He turned his head and stared straight at her. The intense disbelief in his eyes was both appealing and sorrowful. She thought he looked like a child who had been beaten and turned from home and now, wearied to death, had lost its way. His lips suddenly moved, quite soundlessly this time, and then as if out of sheer fatigue stayed loosely open.

He knew now that she was there. He seemed to be trying, she thought, to say something to her. It might have been that he was ill or merely trying to ask the way, but whatever it was she no longer felt an atom of fear. Instead she even released her hold on the hook, climbed a step or two down the ladder and called to him:

'Is there something you want? Can I help you?'

'I'm looking for this place,' he started to say. 'This –'

His voice was cultured, more firm than she had expected but so low that she only just caught the words.

'What place?' she said. 'This is the last house up here – '

'It's up this lane. Somewhere. I think it is. I'm pretty sure – '

'This lane doesn't go anywhere. It's a dead-end. There's no through way.'

'I think it's here – somewhere up here – '

'Place? What kind of place? A house? Are you sure you've come the right way?'

His head moved convulsively, so that he almost dropped the box. Then he retrieved it and clutched it more tightly than ever and said:

'It's a primrose place. You know. A wood. Full of primroses. Thousands of them.'

Now, she thought, she knew. She had been wrong about him all the time. She was now aware that she was dealing with a madman. The eyes were imbecilic; they were neither sorrowful nor weary. Her fear came searing back in a lacerating whirl and she gripped the hook fiercely again and hid her face behind the trunk of the tree.

'You can't walk without stepping on them. Thousands of them. Millions – '

'Will you go away?' She suddenly shouted the words in panic. 'There aren't any primroses. Don't you know? Not now. Not this time of year ! – '

'I never stop seeing them. It's here – somewhere.'

Her throat tightened coldly. She looked wildly up and down the lane, hoping that someone might be passing, but there wasn't a soul in sight. On the very crest of the hillside the colours of autumn flared in gold and orange pyres from great woods of oak and beech. All along the lane the hedge-row lines, yellow and purple and brown, were here and there skeined with berries bright as blood. The unbroken autumn stillness of mid-afternoon seemed to hold her in a trap, the air clenched and sinister.

Her next thought was of the telephone. She would make a dash across the orchard and through the garden and into the house and get to the telephone. She seemed actually to hear herself screaming into it that there was a madman in the garden, escaped from somewhere, muttering insanely about primroses, searching for some idiotic primrose place that wasn't there.

Then suddenly it all seemed unreal and impossible. She was no more than a stricken rabbit. Even if she got to the bottom of the ladder she would never make the garden gate. Then she heard him say:

'Don't you really know this place? I've come an awful way. Walked every bit of it.'

'I don't know any place. There's no place of that sort here.'

'There aren't many big trees. Mostly hazel I think. And a path going through. And primroses all the way. Everywhere.'

A thread of coherence in all this slightly lessened her fear. His hands trembled visibly again and for the second time he almost dropped the box. Then for some reason she suddenly felt unaccountably sorry for him. She realized now that he had hardly strength enough to hold the box, let alone attack her if she ran.

'Will you go if I get you some tea?' she said.

He looked vaguely away from her, up the lane, as if he hadn't heard. Almost involuntarily she started slowly to climb down the ladder, her legs stiff from standing on it so long. Half way down she remembered that she hadn't got the hook and it gave her the strangest feeling of being white and naked.

Then abruptly he walked away. Suddenly it was altogether as if he'd never been there. It was all a grotesque illusion, a mid-afternoon nightmare. Then she saw that once again she was mistaken about him. He hadn't walked away at all. He had simply fallen soundlessly backwards on the roadside verge.

When she got to him he was lying awkwardly on his back. Like a man in a fit he was staring upwards, eyes wide open but sightless. His hands still gripped the box, looking incredibly like two damp white frogs against the blackness of the wood.

The fear leapt wildly through her mind that he was dead. She was half-ready to scream when one of the hands moved slightly and the flicker of a sigh crossed his mouth.

'Don't move,' she said. 'I'll get a rug and some aspirin –'

'Where's the box? Have I got the box?'

'It's all right. Stay there. I'll get some water and some aspirin.'

'God,' he said and shut his eyes. 'Jesus –'

When she got back from the house, three or four minutes later, with a rug and a bottle of aspirins and a glass of water, he was making the feeblest of efforts to sit up. She saw that he hadn't even the strength to raise his head more than an inch or so off the grass and she knelt down and lifted him into a half-sitting position and gave him a sip or two of water. Then she dropped the rug over his knees and said:

'You fainted, I think. I'll get some tea in a minute. Take it quietly.'

He seemed to revive a little after that and said, very slowly:

'I expect you probably think I'm mad.'

'No, no. Take it quietly.'

'Is the box all right?'

'Yes, yes. Don't worry about the box. Could you swallow some aspirin now?'

He gave the slightest nod of his head. He was able now to sit up a little more of his own accord and presently, with hardly a tremor of his hands, he took a couple of aspirins.

'I'm sorry about all this,' he said. He suddenly looked extraordinarily boyish, his fair hair wet at the forelock with the sweat of weakness, his whole appearance shamefaced. 'I don't think I realized quite how far I'd come.'

'Don't worry about that.'

'I've been out of my mind for a week or more. I know that.'

She begged him not to talk about it. Would he come into the house? She experienced not the slightest spasm of fear now. Could he manage it? She'd get some tea. She could do with a cup herself.

'I ought to get on,' he said. 'I've come such a hell of a way. No, thanks all the same, I won't come in.'

He shook his head sharply from side to side, as if in an effort to shake it free of final numbness, and said something about having to get it over with. He'd feel better about things once he'd got it over.

'What are you looking for?' she said. 'Where are you trying to go?'

'We'd been married a year. Just under. Where? It's just this wood, you see. I know it's here – somewhere here. It was the April after we were married. I know because we went through a place called Worten. It stuck in my mind. Is there a place called Worten here?'

'Yes, there's a place called Worten. Down the hill there.'

'Then this must be it. Yes, we left the car somewhere down there and then walked.'

He lifted the glass of water and took a fairly steady drink. Had he walked here today? she said, and he said yes, he'd walked, all the way, all thirty odd miles of it. He'd never drive a car again.

'I felt sort of light-headed when I first saw you. Didn't quite know what I was doing. I'm sorry about all that. I must have frightened you.'

'What do you mean about primroses?'

'Oh! that's the place.'

'But not at this time of year.'

'Oh! no, no. I know that.'

He stopped talking, took another sip or two of water and then stared hard at her, first at her hands and then at her face.

'You're not married, are you?'

'No. I live here with my sister. She's out today. We sort of run it as a bit of a market garden.'

'Nice spot.'

He suddenly surprised her by getting abruptly to his feet,

going to the orchard gate and leaning on it, staring through the apple trees to the red-tiled, white-board house beyond. Now, for the first time, she was looking at him from behind and her surprise at seeing a six-inch strip of plaster running from the base of his skull to the nape of his neck was so great that she almost cried out. But before she could utter a sound he turned and said:

'Sort of place we wanted. Just the thing. Never found it, though.'

He looked ill again, she thought, his face ashen. Wouldn't he come into the house for a bit? It was easy to make some tea.

'No, no,' he said. 'No, thanks, really.'

Involuntarily he lifted a hand and touched the back of his head as if he felt some pain there.

'That looks nasty,' she said. 'How – '

'Crash. Lost my memory for a bit.'

So perhaps, after all, she had been right about him. The memory and perhaps the brain too had gone a little. That, she thought, might account for it all.

'You really should take it easy. You should lie down for a while.'

'Easy?' There was the slightest touch of mockery about the word. 'Oh! yes. Easy. Like doing a dice – easy. At the time. It's when it catches up with you.'

From mockery the tone of his voice sharpened to bitterness. She was at a loss for anything to say. Instead she picked up the rug from where it had fallen on the grass and began to fold it carefully.

'Easy. One minute you're doing a hundred and ten. The next you don't remember anything. Then you wake up and somebody's dead. But not you. Oh! no, not you.'

He abruptly stopped talking again and stared at her in a trance of stricken silence. Again she was utterly at a loss for anything to say. She found it hard, too, even to look at his face, mute and mentally hurt. She found herself simply staring at the box instead.

Suddenly he came out of the trance and said, slowly and with great difficulty:

'They wanted to know if I would have her name or initials or something on it. But I couldn't have that. Have you ever been into one of those places? They play canned music – just canned music – '

It came to her suddenly what was in the box. A cold crust formed at the back of her neck and slowly slid down her spine.

'It seems they always offer them to you. I didn't know that before.'

All she could think of saying was to make once again the now pointless and almost fatuous suggestion about making some tea. He saved her from doing this by saying:

'I'm sure you know this place. This primrose place, I mean. It's right at the top there. Where the road ends.'

'Yes,' she said. 'I know the place. I know now where you mean. Yes, it's where the road ends.'

He started muttering disjointedly, saying that he ought to get on. He said something too about the brilliance of an April afternoon, the light of it and the magic. You might have thought the primroses were pools of yellow water. A marvellous place. Absolutely the place.

'If you cared to call in on your way back – '

'No,' he said. 'Thank you all the same. I'll get on now.'

He muttered good-bye and turned sharply away from her. She said good-bye too. Without another word he walked away up the lane, slowly, not once looking back.

For several minutes' longer she watched him walking up between the lines of the hedgerows, between flaring yellow walls of maple and skeins of berries brilliant as blood, until at last he disappeared, the fair head lost under the great consuming pyres of leaves.

Shandy Lil

I REMEMBER a July afternoon in my Uncle Silas' garden when the raspberries were as big as walnuts and very nearly black. Where sun and shade met on the edge of the hazel spinney a line quivered all afternoon like pure white fire and far and deep under the trees the shade was black too.

We were supposed to be gathering raspberries for jam-making, but I was eating most of mine as I picked them and Silas wasn't working very hard either. He was lying flat on his back between the tall dark rows of canes with his head on his rolled-up jacket and a soft straw hat on his face. Now and then he lifted up the rim of the straw hat like a trap door and dropped a raspberry into his mouth, smacking his wet red lips with the sound of a clapper.

'These 'ere raspberries remind me of Pikey Willis,' he said. 'Can't jistly recollect if I ever told you about Pikey, did I?'

No, I said, I had never heard of this Pikey.

'Big man,' my Uncle Silas said. 'Onaccountable big an' red. Very hairy too. Looked as if he'd got half a sheaf o' barley growing on the backs of his hands. Had a big red beard too. Just like a fox's brush dangling on his chops.'

After this he popped another raspberry into his mouth and shook his head thoughtfully and then surprised me by saying that he'd always felt onaccountable sorry for Pikey.

'Very strong man, Pikey,' he said. 'Could lift a twenty score sow wi' one hand.'

I didn't say a solitary word to this, largely because it seemed to me I had heard something remarkably like it before. In a moment, I felt, I should be listening to the epic history of how my Uncle Silas had floored Pikey, the big boaster, in a wrestling bout, had beaten him cold with raw fists in a fight of fifty rounds or had put him under the table

74

in a beer-drinking match after swallowing half a dozen barrels.

Instead I had another surprise.

'Very nice chap, Pikey,' my Uncle Silas said. 'Very quiet. Onaccountable shy and timid. Allus blushin'. Might have been a gal.'

With a smack of his lips he popped another raspberry into his mouth and at the same time I remembered something. What about the raspberries? I said. What had they to do with Pikey?

'I wur comin' to that,' he said, 'if you'll let me git me breath.'

And what was the reason, I said, for being sorry for Pikey?

'I wur comin' to that an' all,' he said, 'if you don't keep a-chivvyin' on me all the time.'

If there was anybody less out of breath and less chivvied at that moment it was my Uncle Silas, lying flat on his back under his soft straw hat in the shade of the raspberry rows.

'You're allus in sich a nation tearing hurry to git on,' he said. 'Pipe down a minute. I'm a-recollectin' on it.'

For the next few minutes, while my Uncle Silas lay sleepily lost in recollection, I lay down myself and stared up at the clear calm blue sky. Presently I heard him give a long slow ripe smack of his lips and say softly:

'Yeller 'uns. Beautiful yeller 'uns they wur.'

Yellow what? I said. I hadn't the faintest notion what he was talking about.

'Raspberries,' he said. 'The raspberries Pikey growed.'

I had to confess I had never heard of yellow raspberries and he he said:

'Best flavour o' the lot. Beautiful an' sweet. Ain't so big, mind you, but lovely and soft. You don't see 'em growed much nowadays.'

For the second time, perhaps a little impatiently, I said I had never heard of yellow raspberries.

'Neither had she,' he said.

And who, I said, was she?

'Shandy Lil,' he said. He smacked his lips again, softly this time, in what I thought was slower, riper, fruitier recollection. 'Shandy Lil.'

And who, I said again, was she?

'Pikey's gal,' he said. 'Any rate the gal he wur arter.'

'What was she like?'

'Never forgit it,' he said with remarkable quickness. 'Allus remember it. Beautiful hot evening. I'd bin a-mowin' a medder all day and I'd knocked down about seventeen pints and wur just orf to *The Swan with Two Nicks* for another quart or two.'

In one quick leap my Uncle Silas was far ahead of me.

'Hardly got five minutes up the medder lane afore I come across Pikey,' he said, 'sitting on 'eap o' stones, trembling like a good 'un.'

At this point I tried to draw my Uncle Silas out by saying, as he so often reminded me himself, that that was just what women did to you, but he ignored this inviting remark completely.

'Nussin' a paper bag,' he said. 'Lookin' jist like a boy as'd bin caught bird's-nestin' and couldn't git rid o' th' eggs. Blushin' an' quiverin' an' quakin' all over.'

Sucking at another raspberry almost black with bloom, he went on to say what a terrible thing it was to see a big strong chap like Pikey in such a nervous state. 'I felt on-accountable sorry for him,' he said, 'and arter a bit I asked him what wur the matter.'

After this he paused for so long that I was about to show my impatience again by asking exactly what was the matter when he lifted the straw hat rather sharply and said:

'It ain't allus the strong 'uns as make a goo on it. Ain't allus the big 'uns. Strength ain't everything.'

A go of what? I asked him. And who with?

'Wimmin,' he said. 'Pikey wadn't gittin' nowhere with that gal. He wur frit to death on her. Bin tryin' to speak to her for weeks. Heart failed him every time.'

What was she like? I asked him again, this time firmly. Pretty?

'Her mother kept a pub over at Nether Dean,' he said with that remarkable quick blandness again, not even lifting the straw hat.

'*The Blacksmith's Arms.* Seems Pikey used to goo over every night and have a pint or two there and stare at this gal across the bar. That's all. Jist stare. Wadn't gittin' nowhere. Never said a word.'

What was she like? I said again. Big? Fair?

'Dammit, man, how do I know what she wur like?' he said. 'I 'adn't set eyes on her yit, 'ad I? I'm still a-sitting on this 'ere 'eap o' stones with Pikey and this goodly bag o' raspberries, ain't I?'

His voice, though juicy, was quite acid and I lay back in silence between the raspberry rows, momentarily subdued.

'I'll outline her in a minute,' he said, 'if you'll hold hard. But I got to git there fust, ain't I?'

In the process of getting there my Uncle Silas dwelt for some time on the pitiful nature of the raspberries in the paper bag. They were Pikey's idea of a present to a girl, a sort of opening offering, but yellow or not, Silas said, they wouldn't do at all.

'"Fust you got wrap everything up, Pikey," I told him. "That's what wimmin like. Surprises. Unwrappin' things. A bit o' mystery. Next you got to roll up to that pub as if you *are* somebody. Git a trap and a spankin' little mare and drive up in that. Tie a bit o' ribbon on her tail and another bit on the whip and put a big Sweet William in your button-hole. You'll never git nowhere crawlin' and tremblin' on your hands and knees. Wimmin don't like that."'

All Pikey could do, it seemed, was to sit on the heap of stones and say, over and over again: 'I dussn't do it, Silas, I dussn't do it. I ain't made that way.'

By this time I had begun to feel quite a bit sorry for Pikey myself. There is nothing quite so touching as a shy, helpless, muscular man.

'What happened?' I said.

'Well,' my Uncle Silas said, 'when a chap don't know how to do his courtin' you best git on and show 'im. That's what I say.'

Accordingly, two nights later, my Uncle Silas borrowed a trap and a little brown mare from a man named Joe Billington and tied a blue and yellow ribbon on the mare's tail and a crimson bow on the whip.

'Pikey picked a beautiful lot o' raspberries and I laid 'em on a nice bed o' leaves in a little bit of a flat basket. Then I covered 'em over with a bit o' white muslin and tied it on with blue ribbon and then slipped a few cornflowers round the handle and tied them on too. Then I put a big red rose in me buttonhole and a big pink and white Sweet William in Pikey's and we spanked off like a couple o' dukes gooin' to the races.'

This time I didn't ask what happened. Somehow I knew that when they got to *The Blacksmith's Arms* Pikey would sit in the trap outside, all of a tremble, and say 'I dussn't do it, Silas, I dussn't do it. I ain't made that way.'

'Said it forty times if he said it once,' my Uncle Silas said. 'Couldn't git him into that bar nohow. Wild horses wouldn't git him in.'

At this point I made the inviting suggestion that my Uncle Silas had naturally had no such misgivings but, reposing blandly under the straw hat, he ignored that invitation too.

'"Pikey," I said, "you sit out here and hold the basket while I goo in an' coax her. I'll coax her the best I can and tell her all about you and arter a bit she'll come out and then *you* can coax her. You can take her up the lane for a ride and gather a bit o' honeysuckle. Beautiful honeysuckle I noticed on the edge o' that spinney back there. Nothing like a bit of honeysuckle for coaxing gals."'

When I asked how long the coaxing had taken and what had happened afterwards my Uncle Silas didn't even bother to raise the rim of his straw hat.

'It wur gittin' a bit dusk when we come out, I know that,' he said. 'It wur still nation hot and the mare wur a bit rest-less. But that wadn't all. Only thing in the trap wur th' basket. Pikey had done a bunk. Chap sittin' outside with his missus having a quart said he'd gone tearin' down the road as if his beard wur a-fire.'

With slow care my Uncle Silas chose himself another raspberry. As he sucked it into his loose red lips it stained them with an almost purple smear.

'Growin' on a very tall hedge, that honeysuckle,' he said. 'Had a job to reach it.'

'What was she like?' I started to say again. 'Dark? What was she –'

'Growin' up a big tall hedge, other side of a big dyke full o' medder-sweet and willer-herb and burnet and all that.'

I didn't ask what she was like any more. For some reason I had made up my mind that she was dark and how nice she would have looked with golden fingers of honeysuckle in her hair.

'They say the best fruit's allus at the top o' the tree,' Silas said. 'So wur that honeysuckle. Too high for me. Couldn't git at it nohow.'

With what I thought was some effort he managed a bit of a sigh.

'Had to lift her up,' he said. 'On'y thing for it. Had to lift her up.'

Then he went on to say how light she was, light as a feather, and how he sat her on his shoulder. At first he clasped her round the legs but she laughed so much she couldn't lift her arms. Then he put his hands round her waist and tried to lift her that way but the honeysuckle was still far out of reach and in the end they both fell down.

'Fust time she fell a-top o' me in the medder-sweet,' he said. 'Then we tried it again and I fell a-top of her.'

He sighed again, as if re-living, I thought, the long July dusk with the honeysuckle, the meadow-sweet and Shandy Lil. But suddenly he said:

"That's why them yeller raspberries allus remind me of her – '

'Oh! damn the raspberries,' I said. 'I know all about the raspberries. What was *she* like, man?'

With solemn slowness he lifted an edge of his straw hat and cocked his eye at me.

'If you goo over to *The Blacksmith's Arms* at Nether Dean,' he said, 'you'll see a gal there behind the bar. That's Shandy's grand-daughter.'

'Anything like her?'

'Spittin' image,' he said. 'Same white skin. Same light brown hair. Colour o' beer but not quite. More like a drop o' Shandy.'

He sighed again and from the spinney a breath of wind stirred the leaves and ran along the raspberry rows, blowing all the ripe fragrance of red-black fruit into the heat of afternoon.

'Beautiful white skin,' he said. 'Beautiful little figure.' He held up a big ripe raspberry and contemplated the firm red cone of it in a musing dream. 'Hadn't got a blemish on her nowhere.'

'Nowhere?'

He chuckled for the last time, ripely.

'Not as far as I could see,' he said, 'but then it wur gittin' dark at the time.'

The Sun of December

'I am so old,' he said, 'that the only way I can get out of a damn taxi is to crawl out backwards, on my hands and knees.'

'You don't look a day older,' I said.

'Than what?' He looked at me with eyes as bright as water forget-me-nots, from under handsome white brows that were like the head feathers of an owl. 'I'm eighty-seven remember.'

'A mere youth.'

'Dammit, Hell,' he said, 'they're talking of putting me in a wheelchair.'

Across the garden, from the terrace along which a few pale violet winter irises were in bloom, delicate as orchids in the December sun, I could see beyond an expanse of marsh-land the bright gold saucer of sun. Over the windless bay a track of low sunlight made an elongated pool of light exactly the colour of the sherry that clung to two of three glasses on a silver tray.

'Not too dry for you?'

The sherry in fact was rather sweet; but before I could answer he said:

'Women never like it dry. I know Mrs Arkwright doesn't.'

'Mrs Arkwright?'

'She'll be coming to lunch,' he said. 'She's a near neighbour of mine.'

I hadn't really been invited to lunch; I had simply dropped in with a few pots of things that I knew he wanted, a fuchsia or two, a house-plant in silver-green that I thought would charm his window.

'I must be going,' I said.

'Oh! Good God, no,' he said. 'Dammit. You're staying

to lunch. You don't come all this way simply to have a glass of sherry and then rush back again.'

'Yes, but – '

'I won't hear of it,' he said. 'What about this house-plant, this trailing thing you brought me? How does it do?'

I said it was probably the easiest thing in the world, especially for a gardener like him, and he said:

'There's a marvellous thing I want to show you down in the peat-garden before you go. See if you know it. I won't tell you what it is.'

He breathed deeply at the air. The day was utterly un-wintry, delicate and soft-breathed, without a touch of malice. Geraniums were still blooming, pale crimson, along the house wall. Below us there were bushes of late yellow roses; a thrush was singing in the woodland.

'Hark at that thrush. By this time last year we'd had snow,' he said. 'In November. I remember pulling back the curtains when I went to bed and there it was like cotton wool on all the trees.'

He leaned forward to pour another glass of sherry but at that moment there was a fluffy sort of cry, fluffy then cracked, from along the terrace. I looked up to see a vision in what at first I thought was a rosy nightgown trimmed with bird-like edges of swansdown. Across the shoulders of it was a fur wrap of vole-brown with a fox-head clasped by a silver chain.

'Wolfie, Wolfie,' she said. 'Dear Wolfie.'

I thought he looked excessively pained when she called him Wolfie. There was a thickish scent of clove carnations in the air. Her umbrella was mauve, with a long black handle, and she was wearing a bunch of violets in the way I remember women wearing them when I was a boy: at the waist and a little to one side.

She kissed him several times on both cheeks, calling him Wolfie again. With great difficulty he had managed to get to his feet and now stood, arthritic, crabbed, and as erect as he could get himself, balancing between the table and the chair.

When he introduced us she seemed so surprised at my being there at all that she could not even smile. She giggled uncertainly instead and said several times:

'What a heavenly day. What a heavenly day to come up here.'

I poured sherry. She sipped it with eagerness, spilling some of it down the uppermost of her three powdery chins. Then when we were all sitting down again she touched the marbled frontal waves of her silver-grey hatless hair. Nothing, I thought, could possibly have disturbed those metallic corrugations but the preening movements of her hand made me aware, for the first time, of her eyes.

They, too, like his own, were very blue.

'Well, don't you notice?' she said to him. 'Don't you notice? Wolfie! – You're a gardener and you don't see the very most important thing about me.'

It was some seconds before he noticed; and then he smiled with apologetic charm.

'Violets,' he said.

'Yes, and *from my garden*,' she said. 'Note that. *From my garden*. In December.'

She bent to touch them, croaking again with cracked and fluffy exclamations.

'Oh! my dear. They've gone already. I got them at ten this morning and they've gone. All flabby and floppy – look at them. No, don't say it, don't say – I know what you're thinking.' She giggled erratically. 'I know what you're thinking – they fade, they fade!'

'Only because,' I said, and the words were out before I could think about them, 'you're wearing them wrong side up.'

'Oh! Wrong what?'

'If you wear them head downwards,' I said, 'the moisture from the stalks runs down to the flowers and they never fade.'

'Well, you learn something every day, don't you?'

If there had been a breath of ice from the sea it could not have chilled me more.

'Mrs Arkwright has a wonderful garden,' he said. 'She is lower down the hill. They're more sheltered there.'

'Oh! Wolfie. You know it's just a mess. You know I haven't got the touch. Things never do for me. They never respond. I haven't got the touch. Not like you. You've only got to *look* at things –'

'I rather think we ought to go in to lunch,' he said.

'What about that *thing* you were going to show me? – you talked about it the other day – something in the peat-garden? I want to see it – I want you to take me down.'

'I ought just to go in and see about the wine,' he said. 'I tell you what – let Mr Richardson take you down. He's a great gardener. You two go down together.'

'Oh! no,' she said. 'It will do after lunch. The sun doesn't go down till four.'

I felt, in fact, that it had gone down at that moment, off the terrace, off the bright buds of the yellow roses and from across the limpid surface of the sea.

We had sweet white wine for lunch. It was too sweet for me and I thought it too sweet, also, for him, but it seemed perfect for Mrs Arkwright, who said:

'Delicious wine. You always find the most delicious wine, Wolfie. We never have wine like this. Never like this – I don't know where you find these things.'

Her face, fired by the wine, began to come out in a series of blotches, especially under the eyes, almost as bright a red as her lipstick.

'And the lamb-chops. I've never had a lamb-chop like this since before the war. I can't think where you get them. We've got a butcher who kills nothing but dogs, and here you get meat like butter.'

I thought his occasional smile at these things, from the old vivid blue eyes, was nothing like as fresh and positive as it had been when he and I, alone on the terrace, had little to talk of but the spring-like air, the singing thrush and the sea.

'Shall we have coffee inside?' he said, 'or shall we brave the terrace?'

'We don't want you to get cold,' she said.

'Dammit,' he said, 'I've been sitting there all morning.'

'Well, anyway, first you have to show me the flower in the peat-garden.'

'Let's have coffee first,' he said. 'Coffee first.'

It was decided, after all, to have coffee on the terrace, and again we sat in the incredible, golden, soft-aired afternoon. A few moments before this Mrs Arkwright left us for the cloakroom, so that for five minutes the two of us were alone again on the terrace, he sitting down, I looking at the gold-grey bay of sea.

'Immense energy,' he kept saying. 'Immense energy. How old would you think she was? She's been married twice. She lost the second about a year ago.'

'Hard to say.'

'Seventy-four. She wouldn't admit it. But I know.'

He kept looking arthritically over his shoulder, with stiff difficulty, as if half-terrified she would hear.

Some moments later I looked at my watch. It was already nearly three o'clock and I said:

'I ought to run along. It's later than – '

'Good God, man, dammit,' he said. 'I don't want you to go yet. You must stay to tea. You've not been over for months and now you rush away.'

When she joined us again there was a smell of new powder in the air. I noticed now that she had pinned her violets up-side down and that their dark heads were wet with water. She didn't look at me very much, but the fox's head did and the lion-brown pupils seemed almost to snarl, I thought, whenever they caught the sun.

'Now the peat-garden,' she said, when we had finished coffee. 'Come on. What *is* this flower?'

It had been a cruel business to get his twisted stiffened

back into a chair at all, and now she hardly seemed to notice that it was an even crueller business to get it out again.

'My dear Lilah,' he said to her at last, 'I can't make it.' He sank back. 'I'm just a damn miserable bone-bag. I can hop like a two year old if I can get on my feet but I can't get on my feet. Dammit, you'll have to let Richardson take you down. I want you both to see it anyway.'

'Oh! Wolfie, you mustn't talk like that.'

'Like what?' he said. 'They're going to put me in a damn wheelchair.'

'Oh! Wolfie – rubbish. Not for a million years. I wouldn't let them.'

'There's damn little you can do about it.'

'Oh! Wolfie,' she said. 'You're not ready for a wheel-chair. You don't look a day older than you did when we first came here two years ago.' She turned to me for one of her rare, bright-eyed, smiling questions. 'You don't think he does, do you?'

'Not a day older.'

'I sometimes feel a hell of a sight older,' he said, 'that's all.'

'What, with eyes like that? With those blue eyes?' she said. 'Oh! Wolfie.'

I finished my coffee and stood up.

'I must say good-bye,' I said.

'Oh! no, but must you?' he said. 'You were going to see that thing in the peat-garden. Don't run off. I've got to take you down.'

'Look,' I said. 'Sit still. I'll go out that way and find it myself.'

'That's a good idea,' she said.

'Tea will only be an hour,' he said. 'It's always at four. Dammit. Surely you can stay for tea?'

'I really ought to go,' I said.

She smiled at me with unexpected ease and sweetness.

'Have you far to go?'

'Ten miles.'

'Oh! quite a way.'

'Well, all I can say is I'm disappointed,' he said. 'I'm disappointed.'

The merest breath of wind, a moment later, blew up from the sea, not cold, but a mere opening and unfolding of a pocket of air that closed almost immediately again, leaving the afternoon as soft as ever.

'Wolfie, it's turning colder,' she said. 'I don't think it's wise for you to be out here on the terrace. I'll tell you what –'

She turned, to my great surprise, to me.

'I'll just run down to the peat-garden with Mr Richardson and see this thing. You get yourself inside.'

'Well, if you must go, good-bye,' he said. 'Come over again soon. Don't let it be so long. Remember I'll have a cyclamen for your wife at Christmas. One of those big frilled white ones that she likes so much –'

'Ah! like the one you promised me?' she said.

In a cloud of carnation scent I followed her down to the peat-garden. The air was beautiful. The sea startled the entire valley with a flash of vivid brassy light. She chatted in a high voice about the day, the garden, the altogether remarkable weather and the fact that it was so nice I was a gardener too.

'Have you any idea what this thing could be?' she said. 'Because I haven't the faintest.'

It turned out to be a little rhododendron, pinkish, wintry, delicate in the dying sun. She looked at it for a second or two indifferently and then said to me, with eagerness, with the brightest of eyes and a prancing scarlet smile:

'Oh! it's been *so* nice to see you. I can't tell you how nice it's been. That's one of the things about Wolfie – his marvellous friends.'

She turned to go back up the path to the terrace. Then she hesitated, remembering something.

'And that was a nice touch about the violets. I never knew. You see, they're already fresh again.'

She gave me a final flash, a little coy, very blue and half-cajoling, of her bright blue eyes.

'You know the way down to the bottom gate, don't you?' she said.

'Yes,' I said. 'I know the way.'

In the second before I turned to go I saw him still standing on the terrace. The spring-soft sunlight of the winter afternoon was bright on his face. He did not lift his hand.

Seeing her turn too, he fled like someone doomed.

The Courtship

I RAN into him on one of those moonless, muggy evenings, a couple of days before Christmas, when the air is like lukewarm stew – or rather, to be truthful, he ran into me. He was pushing a sizeable hand-truck loaded with flowers: all sorts of them, mostly in pots, azaleas, hyacinths, narcissi, cyclamen, tulips, and several bunches of yellow mimosa, all fresh and fluffy.

It was not merely that the street was exceptionally dark there or that the truck was exceptionally heavy. He himself seemed almost sightless, unaware of where he was going. The truck seemed to lurch at me as I was about to step off the pavement and I just saved myself in time by clutching the side of it.

The damp winter air was full of half a dozen fragrances as he stood there panting, absent-eyed, muttering something about being sorry. He seemed, I thought, about sixty and he coughed heavily several times, struggling to get his breath.

I couldn't give him a pound, he supposed, could I? – and for a moment I thought he was talking of money. Then I realized that we were on a sharp incline and that he was talking of pushing the truck.

'Going far?' I said.

It was three or four streets away, he said, not more than half a mile. His voice was husky. Phlegm seemed to be choking his throat, so that whenever he opened his mouth the words came out all broken up, even the syllables severed apart. His eyes groped in the damp lamp-lit distances in the same broken way and he seemed to be trying to focus, in the stony darkness, some object far beyond them.

'Got to take 'em just past *The King's Arms* in Victoria Road,' he said. 'Know where I mean?'

I said I did. A moment later my hand was on the truck and presently, side by side, we were pushing it away.

As we moved into lighter parts of the street the thing that struck me most about him was not his eyes or his hands or that huskily broken voice of his. It was his nose. It was exactly like an old potato.

Not just a plain old potato, either, but one that had been baked in its jacket, pinched about a bit, left to get cold and consequently looked terribly rough, misshapen and sad. His hair was equally unbeautiful. It was matted, stiff and grey, looking more than anything else like an old wire-haired terrier's ear that at some time or other had been rudely mangled in a fight. Sometimes he lifted a hand as if to ruffle the hair but the gesture always ended abruptly and in the same way: he gave a sudden jab with his thumb at the side of the old potato.

I don't want to give the impression here that what he subsequently had to tell me presented itself in an easy, fluent rush. It came out in a typically broken way, in bits and pieces. It was for me almost entirely a matter of picking up echoes and half clues, muttered and difficult snaps of memory failing in the darkness.

'Bill Browning,' he said and then, half a minute later, as if he had entirely forgotten it, said it again. 'Bill Browning. That's me.'

He was living, it seemed, all alone, in one room, with a bed, a gas-fire and a meter. The bed – I saw it later – looked as if it had been built from old bicycle frames and he had slept in it for thirty years.

That was some time, I gathered, before he met a girl named Edna. It seemed that he was forty, perhaps more, before he began to court her. She was over forty too but he thought of her then, and for ever afterwards, as a girl. She worked in a wholesale clothing factory and later, when he showed me a picture of her, I could see that, like Bill, she wasn't very much to look at. She was smallish and rather mild looking, with pale, indeterminate eyes, nondescript hair and a face whose complexion, I guessed, could have been of a kind of parsnip shade. Somehow I could see her wearing hats five or six years out of date, old fashioned corsets of the sort that creak and plain black lace-up shoes that probably pinched her.

Without doubt Bill thought her very beautiful and equally without doubt, I fancied, she thought him beautiful too. The pair of them were locked in mutual devotion and they met on regular nights, every Saturday, Sunday, Tuesday and Thursday. I seemed to see them meeting on some secluded corner somewhere, she with a springy walk in the tight black shoes and Bill, as he waited, rubbing his thumb in nervous anticipation against the old potato.

All this time he was working as an odd-job man for a firm of grocer's and when he was just over forty they gave him a raise. It wasn't very much of a raise but the extra four shillings prompted him to ask if Edna, perhaps, would marry him. Edna said she was thrilled and would love to but it couldn't very well be, anyway not just yet.

'Why?' Bill wanted to know.

It was because of her mother, Edna explained. Her mother had a poorish heart, was seventy and couldn't do much for herself. Edna conceived it not only her duty to look after her; she had actually promised her father as much before he died. She was a cautious girl to whom conscience meant a great deal. She wanted to be true to her word.

'She could come and live with us,' Bill said. 'That wouldn't worry me. I wouldn't mind.'

No. Edna was quite firm about that. That sort of thing never worked out. She knew two other girls who had gone to live with their in-laws and yet another who had her husband's mother living in one room with her and sharing the kitchen. It was just a cat-and-dog life. It never worked out.

Bill, disappointed, even upset – I seemed to see him begin

to rub his rough potato nose with his thumb, as he always seemed to do in moments of emotion or uncertainty – said something about the future didn't seem to hold very much for them, did it, like that?

'I don't want to seem cruel,' Edna said, 'but I don't somehow think she'll live all that long. She has terrible bad turns every so often. I don't want to lose her but really I don't think we'd have to wait all that long while.'

Bill, to whom Edna was obviously his first consideration always, was too good-natured to say that he hoped not. He supposed they'd just have to wait, was all he said, but apparently a note of such disappointment as to be almost sepulchral must have been so sharply marked in his voice that Edna actually stopped suddenly in the street where they were walking, clasped him hard with both hands and said with what I gathered was quite uncharacteristic vehemence, almost passion, that it would be the same for both of them. They'd still have each other.

'I don't mind waiting,' she said. 'I'll wait for ever.'

The four shillings raise had seemed so much part of his plan for Edna and his future that presently Bill began, in a curious way, to be troubled about it. He actually began to feel selfish. He felt that he wanted to confer on Edna the benefit of his raise, or part of it, without positively thrusting the money into her hands. Somehow he wanted to make a gesture of some sort that would compensate her for waiting.

But finally, on a cold November Saturday night, he actually did thrust the money into her hands; all four shillings of it, saying at the same time, while probably rubbing his potato nose hard with his thumb, that he sort of wanted her to treat herself. Perhaps there was some little thing –

'I don't want anything,' Edna said. 'Not a thing. You save your money. We'll need it one day.'

'No,' Bill said and again I guessed he was too considerate, altogether too good-natured, to say what he was thinking –

that one day might never come. 'I want you to have a treat. Now.'

'What sort of treat? What could I buy?'

It suddenly came to Bill as an almost desperate thought that she might, perhaps, buy herself some fish-and-chips.

'At Albert's,' he said. Albert's was five or six doors beyond the terrace house where Edna lived with her mother. Its windows steamed with strong fishy clouds until late into the night. 'They'd be nice and hot if you took them straight in.'

'Well, I don't really – '

'Please,' Bill said and again I seemed to see him rubbing his old potato nose hard, in complexity. 'I want you to. It would sort of even things up.'

'Even things up?' Edna said. She didn't know what he meant.

Nor, in fact, did Bill. Apparently he could only blurt out, in his great eagerness to please, that he would even go into the shop and get the fish-and-chips for her himself.

'No,' Edna said. 'It's very sweet of you but I'll get them.' I seemed to see them at the corner of the street now, fifty or sixty yards from the steaming fish-shop windows. I could imagine a light cold fog coming down and that perhaps Edna was clutching at her coat collar, tilting her face. 'Let's say good night here, shall we?'

'I always come as far as the house – '

'Let's say good night here,' Edna said. 'Old mother Parker was having a good look at us the other night. I saw the curtains move. I don't like being spied on when I kiss you.'

After that, every Saturday night, winter, spring, autumn and summer, Bill gave Edna his four shillings, kissed her good night at the street corner and then watched her, with tender consideration, depart for fish-shop and home.

This simple act of generosity not only became a habit as satisfying in itself as an evening prayer might have been to

another person; it became a means of fortifying him in court-
ship, in what were to be the long years of waiting for Edna.

As a result it seemed hardly any time at all before he and
Edna were fifty. He himself didn't feel much older at fifty,
I gathered, than he had done at forty and I rather suspected
that the only change in his appearance was probably that
his hair, greyer by this time, looked rather more dog-eared
and his nose slightly enlarged, rougher skinned and more
sadly misshapen than ever. Edna, I fancied, looked hardly
any older herself and in another photograph the only change
I could detect in her appearance was that she was obviously
rather plumper about the chin, hips and bust. I could only
guess that this extra weight might have caused her shoes to
pinch a little more, so that she perhaps walked a little more
springily.

Now whenever he went to meet her Bill was filled with
the remotely uncharitable hope that one evening he would
see a change in her. There would come an evening when she
would be walking droopily, perhaps even in tears, or perhaps
even running towards him with outstretched arms, and it
would mean that her mother was dead.

But as the years went by – and in the strange way that time
seems to have they probably appeared to go by much faster
– there was never any change in her step. She continued
to meet him always in the same way and to depart, every
Saturday evening, towards distant clouds of fishy steam.

And soon, as they progressed from their early fifties into
middle fifties, it seemed that the subject of marriage was
hardly ever mentioned. It hardly seemed to matter. The
mere habit of meeting, being with each other, drinking a
glass of stout together in *The King's Arms*, holding each
other's hands in a cinema, walking home and finally kissing
good night became a pattern that was not only satisfactory
in itself. It was consolatory.

So much so that I gathered that Bill sometimes found
himself thinking with foreboding of what might happen if
Edna's mother did die. You never knew, he hinted, with

marriage: it was a funny thing. Not only that, he'd probably have to do something about his one room and its gas fire. That would hardly do for Edna. He would have to change all that. And most of all, I gathered, he had a strange idea that marriage might change Edna. She would sort of grow up. She wouldn't be his girl any more.

And then, one late October evening, at the time when darkness had started to close in early, she wasn't there at the corner when he went to meet her. It was the first time it had happened, I gathered, in more than fifteen years.

For a time he paced up and down a bit and then, presently, began to worry. After nearly an hour he started to be really troubled and he set out to walk to the little terrace house where Edna and her mother lived, between the fried fish-shop and *The King's Arms*.

It took him some time to grasp, I think, that the blinds of the house were drawn. Even when he did so he still paced nervously up and down for some time longer outside, confessedly as agitated at the idea of Edna's mother dying at long last as he would have been at the reality of leading Edna to the altar.

Finally he rapped the knocker of the door. It was some time before the door opened and when at last it did open Edna's mother was there.

'She'd gone,' Bill said to me. His voice broke completely now. 'Edna, I mean. That morning. She was bad just two or three hours, that's all, and then – '

He followed her mother into the house. She kept crying all the time, apologizing over and over again that she hadn't sent him a message. She would have come down herself to tell him, she kept saying, but she didn't like to leave the girl alone.

Bill, too stunned to say much, presently managed to mutter that he thought he'd walk home. He'd perhaps get over it a bit if he started walking. Then, just as he reached the street door, she called him back, weeping again that she was a forgetful fool.

'She wanted you to have this,' she said. He found himself with a large black handbag in his hands. He remembered it as one Edna had had ten years before.

'This? What's this?'

'I never asked her. I never looked inside. She said you was to have it, that's all.'

In a complete daze he walked back to his room with the bag. He sat down on the bed and gazed at the bag for some time before opening it and looking inside.

'It was all in a big envelope,' he told me. 'Every penny.' Edna had written a little note of explanation about it. She was sorry she hadn't spent it and she hoped he wouldn't mind. 'All the fish-and-chip money. About a hundred and eighty quid.'

'She always hated wreaths.' After he had unloaded all the flowers and taken them through the front door of the little terrace house – the blinds at the windows were still drawn – we sat for an hour or two in the bar of *The King's Arms*, Bill steadfastly taking meagre sips of whisky. Now and then he made that abrupt and troubled gesture of rubbing his thumb against his old potato, confessing two or three times that he'd been sleeping bad. 'Terrible bad. Perhaps I'll be better now I've got her the flowers.'

He sat for some time longer, over more whisky, explaining about the flowers. He said again how he wanted to even things up – did I understand? He'd given her that raise of his all that long time ago and she'd put it all away. There'd been no pleasure for her. She'd got nothing out of it. Nothing. Not even a bag of chips.

'I bought about twenty quids' worth,' he said. His eyes, perhaps because of the whisky, were covered with a gentle film. 'The young lady at the flower shop said I'd need a truck. They couldn't deliver – bit difficult at Christmas time. No trouble about that, I told her. I could borrow one from work.'

He was silent for some moments after that and then he

fumbled in his pockets and brought out the first of the pictures of Edna.

'Nice looking girl,' he said. 'Very pretty. Don't you think she's pretty?'

I looked at Edna's mild-looking face, with its nondescript hair and the complexion that I thought must be of a parsnip shade, and said yes, she was very pretty.

'Come in for a minute?' Bill said. We were home now. 'I got half a bottle of whisky inside. Had to get it. Helped me on a bit.'

I went inside with him, into the one room with the gas-fire, the meter and the bed that looked so much as if it had been built from ancient bicycle frames. Another picture of Edna, the one when she was plumper, hung on one wall and below it, on a shelf above the bed, stood a single white hyacinth in a pot. It glowed wonderfully waxy in the light of the gas-lamp Bill had lit and the room was full of the scent of it.

Bill poured the whisky. I stood for some moments staring into my glass, not knowing what to say. It was almost on my lips to say 'Happy Christmas', but I checked myself in time and said simply:

'Here's to you, Bill. And to Edna.'

He didn't speak. The inevitable gesture of rubbing his thumb against his old potato had suddenly the strangest effect on his face. It actually unlocked a smile: making it seem, as it had done to Edna, almost beautiful.

'Thanks. I'm glad I ran into you. Been nice talking. Hardly said a word to a soul since it happened. Did me good to get it off my chest.'

A few minutes later I said good night to him, at the same time telling him how I hoped he'd sleep much better now.

'Thanks,' he said again. We shook hands. 'I got a feeling I will. I feel better now I've given her the flowers. It's sort of evened it up. Bit difficult to understand, I know, but – '

I said I understood and a moment later, as I put my hand on the doorknob, ready to go, he stopped me.

'Have this,' he said. 'I'd like you to have this.'

He was thrusting the white hyacinth into my hands. I started to protest. I felt I couldn't bear to see the little room with its gas-ring, its meter and the old bicycle bedstead to be deprived of the blessing of its only Christmas flower. But Bill, actually raising another smile, insisted and wouldn't hear me.

'You take it. You have it. It's a little gift. For Edna's sake. Eh? For Christmas. I want you to. It would sort of, you know, make me – ' I thought he was about to say happy, but he broke off and said, 'Well, lift me up a bit', instead.

I took the hyacinth and went downstairs and into the street. I carried the flower in front of me, carefully, holding it in both hands. It was exactly like a steadfast fragrant candle, pure and white as snow, lighting the outer darkness.

A Teetotal Tale

'Fust started to drink beer when I wur three,' my Uncle Silas said. 'Not all that big amount, mind you. Jist a pint for breakfast.'

I confess it didn't surprise me very greatly that my Uncle Silas had set himself so early an example in the matter of drinking and I merely remarked, half to myself, in a casual sort of way, how useful that early training had turned out to be, since he'd been going at it with unbroken relish ever since.

'Jist wheer you're wrong, boy,' he said. 'Jist wheer you're wrong.'

A rather worried and melancholy look came over his face as he said this: a mere glimmer of uncertainty, but significant. At the same time he wiped a small drop of moisture from his bloodshot eye and gave a mumbling sort of sigh, letting up a little wind.

'You're not trying to tell me,' I said, 'that you gave it up at some time or other?'

Before answering he leaned back against the haystack where we had been sitting all afternoon and stared at the sky, blue and feathered with late May cloud above the masses of high yellow oak flowers that crowned the spinney. Between us stood a clothes basket full of cowslips, wilting in the genial warmth of afternoon. For over an hour we had been de-flowering the golden-fingered heads and laying them out on an ebony coloured tray to dry.

'Gospel truth,' he said. 'I give it up once, boy. Good and proper. Strike me down if I tell a lie. I went teetotal.'

'For how long?' I said. 'Five minutes?'

My Uncle Silas ignored me dreamily and for some moments longer went on de-flowering one cowslip after another. The weight of memory seemed to bear down on him rather heavily, I thought, but finally he struck one knee of his corduroys with a stern and solemn palm.

'Prit near two months,' he said. 'Gospel. True as I'm a-sittin' here aside this 'ere hay-stack. Prit near two months, boy. Teetotal.'

I remarked that it was a great wonder how he'd ever managed to survive the ordeal, but for nearly a minute he ignored that too. When he spoke again his eye was on the sky.

'It damn well wur an' all,' he said. 'Prit near the death on me.'

After this the melancholy look came back to his face again and he gave another rather worried, weighty sigh.

'It wur cruel,' he said. 'Wuss'n being chained up. Wuss'n a nightmare.'

I started trying to think of some possible explanation to account for this extraordinary lapse on my Uncle Silas's part and it came to me without difficulty.

'Nothing to do with women, I suppose?'

My Uncle Silas slowly de-flowered another cowslip.

'Two on 'em,' he said. 'They got round me, boy. They got round me. Two on 'em. Gal and her mother.'

The notion of anyone getting round my Uncle Silas, still less putting him off his beer for two months, was almost too much to bear. I couldn't speak a word.

'Beautiful gal an' all,' he said. 'Beautiful.'

He paused and held a pensive hand above the cowslips.

'Ever seen a big ripe pear 'anging in a muslin bag?'

I said of course I had. That was the way my Uncle Silas had the big golden Williams hanging every September on the house wall.

'Jist like that she wur,' he said. 'Firm and ripe. Like a nice ripe pear in a muslin bag.'

'All ready for you to pick.'

He took up another cowslip. Then, instead of de-flowering it, he put it in his mouth and started reflectively chewing on the pale green stalk.

'That's about what I thought,' he said.

Cuckoos had been calling across the meadows all afternoon and now one flew over the haystack, chased by two more. My Uncle Silas watched them disappear beyond the oak tree with a bleary eye.

'Fust met her at a fair,' he said. 'Allus remember her. In a white muslin dress and a big white straw hat. Trying to win a clock on the hoop-la.'

'With Ma?'

'With Ma,' he said. He seemed to brighten a little, I thought, at the mention of Ma. A sprightlier glint came back to his eye. 'Ma wur a good looker too, mind you. And only about thirty-five.'

'Another pear?' I said.

'No,' he said. 'She wur more like a big yeller rose. A bit full blown.'

Still chewing at the cowslip stalk, he went on to tell me what a poor mess the girl and her mother were making of the hoop-la and how, pretty soon, he was helping to put this right.

'In about half hour I'd got 'em a clock and all sorts o' fancy bits-o'-kit like vases and dolls and mustard-pots and milk jugs and looking glasses and I don't know what. It wur a warmish day and by the time I'd got 'em loaded well up I started to think it might be a good idea to have a wet or two at *The Rose and Crown*.'

He laughed for the first time that afternoon and the cowslip fell out of his mouth as if in surprise.

'You mighta thought I'd suggested stranglin' the pair on 'em,' he said. 'Ma went white with 'orrer. The gal – Arabella her name wur – said "We do *not* drink, thank you. We have seen enough of *that*." And in a lot less time than it takes to git a pint down they wur gone.'

With renewed sadness my Uncle Silas started to de-flower another cowslip.

'Well, I couldn't git this 'ere gal outa my mind,' he said. 'You know how it gits, boy. They start 'auntin' on you.'

They lived in a keeper's cottage on the edge of the wood, the girl and her mother, he went on, and pretty soon he was trying to court her there. He didn't have all that lot of luck at first and it took him a week or more to find out why, in his own words, 'they were so darnation ostropolus about a little thing like beer'.

Then he found out that the girl's father, a gamekeeper, had got as far as having D.T's about every three or four weeks and was now resting in a home for drunks on the other side of the county.

'If you are coming to see Arabella,' the mother said, 'there must be no drink. Absolutely no drink. No talk of drink. We've been through purgatory enough already.'

'Not half as much as I went through in the next five or six weeks, though, I'll tell you,' my Uncle Silas said. 'Wust time I ever remember. Terrible. Like being in a desert. Thought I'd go mad.'

'But the girl,' I suggested, 'was nice? She was worth it?'

With thoughtful melancholy my Uncle Silas started to de-flower another cowslip.

'That wur the trouble,' he said. 'I wadn't gittin' much fur me money either.'

I found it hard to reconcile this remark with my Uncle Silas' repeated description of the girl as a big juicy pear ripe for picking and I had actually started to say so when he pulled me up quite sharply.

'Ah! but you forgit Ma,' he said. 'Ma was allus there.'

In the parlour, in the kitchen, in the garden, in the woods, across the meadows – Ma, it seemed, was always there.

'Never went quite so far as smelling me breath,' Silas said, 'but that wur the rough idea. I be damned if I could ever git the gal alone.'

I could hardly believe that my Uncle Silas had utterly

failed to find a way of removing the final obstacle to this frustrating state of affairs and I was quite relieved to hear him say:

'Then I had a bit of inspiration. Bit of a brainwave. Very like it wur this teetotal business keepin' me 'ead oncommon clear for a week or two, but suddenly it come over me all of a pop what was up with Ma.'

I ran my hand through the clothes' basket and picked out a handful of juicy cowslip stems, at the same time watching Silas with an inquiring, crucial eye.

'Jealous,' he said. 'That wur the trouble with Ma.'

Philosophically chewing on another cowslip stem, Silas expanded a little further on the theme that there are mothers who are sometimes uncommonly jealous of their handsome daughters.

'Arter all it wur a bit lonely for her,' he said. 'With 'im not there and she only thirty-five. Got to remember that.' I started to inquire how far this interesting discovery had carried him and he laughed for the second time that afternoon and said:

'Arter that it wur easy. Plain sailing all the way. Decided I'd give it up. Rather have the beer than the gal. Hadn't got the gal anyway.'

This seemed, I thought, rather a disappointing end to an episode that I felt would itself ripen like a pear, but my Uncle Silas hadn't finished yet.

'One night I decided I'd nip off home and never come back,' he said, 'but at the last minute I hadn't the heart to tell the gal. Damn it, she wur a beautiful gal, she wur.'

Picking up another handful of cowslips, he went on to tell me how he said good night to the girl and her mother for the last time. It was summer and for some time after leaving there he walked up and down in the lane outside. 'I wanted that gal very much,' he said, and at last he could bear it no longer. He decided to go back to the house and see if he couldn't talk to her alone.

'They were both in bed by that time,' he said, 'and I had to git a ladder and prop it up aside the house so as I could wake her.'

He tapped softly on the window several times and called, 'Arabella' and at last a figure in a white nightgown appeared.

'Arabella,' he said, 'I've got summat I must say to you.'

'It's not Arabella,' a voice whispered, 'it's me.'

My Uncle Silas was never one to lose his head on such occasions and he said quickly:

'Ma, I jist wanted to tell Arabella I shan't be coming this way no more.'

My Uncle Silas laughed softly.

'Thought she'd a fell outa the winder when I said that,' he went on. 'Thought she'd a shed a tear.'

'Upset?'

'Terrible. Couldn't pacify her. Went on summat chronic – about how they liked me so much and how they'd miss me and all that. I wur so surprised I nearly fell off the damn ladder.'

'Instead?'

He laughed softly again.

'She said wouldn't I come into the bedroom a minute and talk it over? So I nipped in for a minute or two.' He was de-flowering cowslips quite fast now, chuckling. 'Matter of fact we talked it over fur the best part o' the night. Very understanding woman she turned out to be.'

'And after that?' I said. 'What about the girl?'

'Well,' my Uncle Silas said, ruminating on the flight of two cuckoos in pursuit above the spinney, 'we come to a sort of pact. I said I'd keep Ma from being too lonely fur a night or two if she'd leave me alone now and then with the gal.'

The cuckoos, calling with throaty bubblings in the warm air, disappeared across the meadows of buttercups, their voices echoing in the still air.

'Very useful ladder that wur,' my Uncle Silas said. 'Up one winder one night and t'other the next.'

I had nothing to say and my Uncle Silas, laughing with a voice as soft and juicy as a full ripe pear, de-flowered another cowslip.

The Picnic

'Now you won't on any account be late for the picnic on Saturday, will you?' Aunt Leonora said. 'I want everybody here as sharp as a packet of pins on the dot of eleven. If your Uncle Freddie's going to get in an hour's fishing before lunch we must make a good early start.'

With casual amiability I always reserved for these charming and unheralded surprises of Aunt Leonora's I inquired to know what picnic?

My aunt and I were sitting in the garden, on the lawn, under the deep shade of a large Blenheim apple tree. It was late June and already the young apples were about the size of walnuts. Many had already fallen but now, as if struck by the winging shrillness of Aunt Leonora's voice, a few more pattered down from the boughs.

'Great Heavens, man,' she said, 'you can't have forgotten the picnic? It was all arranged the very last time you were here.'

It was a typical blatant, thundering lie. I knew of no such picnic. I knew that none had ever been arranged. That a picnic obviously existed in the mind of Aunt Leonora I knew beyond all possible doubt, just as I knew that for her a lie was the truth provided she thought it up fast enough.

'I don't think,' I said, 'I could have been here when you arranged it.'

'Not here? You hear that, Freddie?' she called. 'What a spoof! He's trying to say he wasn't here when we arranged the picnic. Of course you were here! We were all sitting exactly where we are now. Freddie, isn't that so?'

Uncle Freddie, rotund, radish-pink and utterly unassertive, lay in a hammock attached to the far side of the apple tree, enjoying his customary zizz in the warmth of the afternoon. He waved, without a word, what might have been a dissentient hand but equally one that didn't care.

'In fact,' she said to me, revealing in the sweetest of smiles those large, long teeth of hers, 'you actually threw out the idea yourself. "Let's have a fishing picnic," you said, "on the Mill Lake. Just like the one we had last year."'

I couldn't help admiring the words 'threw out'. They had a marvellous casual cunning of their own. They almost had me believing, for one moment, that I had actually concocted this myth of picnics, even the one from last year.

'Moreover you promised to bring that girl – that rather jolly one – what is her name? Penelope.'

With amiable restraint I begged to inform Aunt Leonora that I knew of no girl named Penelope.

'Well, it's a name of that sort. Something like it.'

'Is it?' I said. 'And when was she last on the scene?'

'Oh! you remember as plain as a pike-staff. You'd been to the point-to-point races on Easter Saturday and you met two girls and brought them along here afterwards. With a young man named Tim or something. Tom it might have been.'

'It so happens that I never go to point-to-point races,' I said. 'I loathe them.'

'Well, you'd been *somewhere*.'

'It was Tim Walters who had been to the point-to-points. I was out for a walk when he stopped and gave me a lift and dropped me here. You were clipping the garden hedge and you asked us in for a glass of red-currant wine.'

'I remember the girls so well!' she suddenly said, with a beautiful, half-absent breeziness. 'The one called Penelope was the jolly one, full of mischief – '

'Her name is Peggy.'

'Very well, Peggy.'

'And she isn't the jolly one. She's the rather shy, thoughtful one.'

'Oh! I thought that was Violet.'

'Valerie,' I said. 'She's the jolly one. She's Tim's sister.'

'Oh! really?' she said. 'I thought they were married.'

'Marrying your sister,' I said, 'isn't generally done.'

'Oh! well, then they should have been. I thought they were admirably suited to each other.'

Aunt Leonora is a divine, lovable crack-pot. Many people are tone-deaf or colour-blind or lacking a sense of humour or smell; in Aunt Leonora there are merely strange fundamental forces at work that prevent her from distinguishing, even remotely, between truth and falsehood, fact and fancy. For these reasons she is also a schemer; she for ever seeks to put things right. If two people are not friends when she thinks they ought to be friends, she will strive indefatigably to make them friends, even to the point of total disaster. When she dies there will be carved on her tomb – or should be – the words *There is a Divinity which shapes our ends, rough-hew them how we will,* and she, I fear, will have been the Divinity. She is the great divine end-shaper of all time.

'Anyway, these are the three people you'd like to come to the picnic, are they?' she said, again with that bland, toothy smile.

It was monstrous. It was also impossible.

'Tim,' I said, 'is in Cape Town. He's taken a job there.'

'But his wife and the other girl will come.'

'Not his wife. His sister.'

'Anyway she's the jolly one.'

'She is not the jolly one.'

'Anyway, they'll come, won't they?'

'I haven't asked them.'

'But good grief, man, you must. You're getting awfully slack, aren't you? I've already asked another young man. There'll be just a nice round six of us.'

'What young man?'

Here Aunt Leonora proceeded to describe, in the vaguest possible terms, a young man she sometimes met at the public library. She thought his name was Bennett or Barnett or something of that sort. Her chief impression of him was that he seemed woefully undernourished. He was distressingly thin. He lacked fresh air. He seemed to read mostly books on engineering or science or kindred subjects and had a rather prominent mole on one cheek or the other and was going rapidly and prematurely bald.

'Any idea of his first name?' I said.

'I rather fancy it's David.'

'It sounds like a man named David Benson I know vaguely. He works in insurance.'

'That's it. Benson.'

'And what, pray, made you ask him?'

In answer she gave me one of those dark, meaningful glares, full of sinister suspicion, that were so typical of her.

'*I thought he ought to be taken out of himself.*'

I was about to suggest that perhaps he didn't want taking out of himself, but finally I decided to let this almost accusative piece of information pass without a word. It was just as well I did so because, a moment later, she broke into what sounded like a concluding twitter of song.

'Well, then, that's just about all fixed. I've asked Mr Benson. You'll ask the girls. Uncle Freddie will see to the rods and tackle. And what would you like to eat?'

'Now?'

'No, no. For the picnic. Freddie!' she suddenly called, 'what sort of food do you fancy for the picnic?'

As if from the end of an invisible telephone line Uncle Freddie replied with remarkable alacrity:

'Pork pie and cucumber salad.'

'Oh! no, that's dull. That's ghastly. That's plain cowardice.'

It seemed to me that at this moment Uncle Freddie, so peremptorily crushed, slipped suddenly deeper into the hammock and the zizz.

'You know what I thought would be *an absolutely marvellous thing*?'

Amiable again, I begged her to tell me.

'I think we should picnic off the land.'

'Good God,' I said.

This unlikely and impractical prospect so alarmed me that

it was some moments before I could remind her that she
hated shooting, hunting and violence of any kind to animals
and birds and that she only tolerated fishing for Uncle
Freddie's sake.

'I really meant picnic off the water,' she said.

'Good God,' I said. 'Not fish?'

'Why not? I was thinking principally of perch. I once
had them in Switzerland. On the lake of Geneva. *Filets de
perche*. With local white wine. Absolutely delicious.'

'But supposing,' I said, 'we don't catch any perch?'

She merely gave me the toothiest of white smiles.

'We'll guard against that eventuality by taking smoked
trout along.'

'Oh,' I said.

Perhaps that was cowardice too but it was all, for the
moment, I could think of to say. Inwardly I felt my heart
grieve for the undernourished Mr Benson. I seemed to see,
in imagination, the jolly, healthy, mischievous figure of
Valerie, a girl whose bouncing frame needed strong susten-
ance if ever a living creature did, sucking on the pale bones
of a four-ounce perch.

'Don't you think,' I said, 'that we shall perhaps need
something more substantial?'

'Oh! that's all arranged,' she said with the most disarming
brightness, 'I'm making a big steak-and-kidney pie. We'll
have it cold. And salads and apricot tarts and things of that
sort. Oh! nobody will starve. It was just that I thought we
ought to have one little touch of the wild.'

'One touch,' I said, 'will undoubtedly make the whole
world kin.'

'What was that? What were you muttering about?'

'Nothing at all. Just thinking aloud.'

'Well, just don't. It's an extremely bad habit. I've told
you before. It's worse than thinking with your eyes.'

A moment later she turned swiftly from these dark
accusations to call yet again to Uncle Freddie:

'Freddie, what do perch eat?'

'Worms.'

'Then you must be up at crack of dawn, don't forget. Digging.'

From the round radishy figure of my Uncle Freddie there came, in answer, one brief sound. It might have been the croaking of a snoozing frog.

By half past eleven on Saturday morning I was lowering, gently and indeed with some reverence, half a dozen bottles of red-currant wine into a shallow pool on the Mill Lake, under the dark shade of an alder tree. The morning had on it a blissful and somnolent bloom, tenderly hazy and without glare. The surface of the lake even reeked with misty steam.

'Where are those two children?' Aunt Leonora demanded, I think perhaps for the third or fourth time and as if she didn't know. 'Lost their way, I shouldn't wonder.'

Aunt Leonora continually sought in other people, but rarely found it, that quality of restless and unflagging energy with which she attacked everything in life from chasing mythical marauders from her garden to making currant wine and custard tarts. 'Those children' were the under-nourished Mr Benson and the shy Peggy Mortimer, who were somewhere bringing up the rear of our fishing column with a large basket-work hamper containing picnic plates, cutlery and food.

Aunt Leonora had enlisted them into this task with blatant deliberation, simply with the unashamed purpose of throwing them together. It was clearly her first move in taking Mr Benson out of himself.

'They get on absolutely splendidly together, don't you think?' she said, airily tossing the first part of the sentence to Valerie Charlesworth and the second to me. 'They sort of went for each other from the word go.'

Again I couldn't help admiring her choice of words. 'They sort of went for each other from the word go' was just another characteristic, charming lie. No two people could ever have ached more not to be left alone together.

'There's a sort of fusion when some people meet,' she said, 'isn't there?'

I didn't bother to answer this but merely winked, sideways, at Valerie Charlesworth. With her extraordinary golden-brown eyes, that had in them some of the hazy languor of the morning air, she winked back at me, but whether in understanding or out of sheer mischievous habit or in secret invitation about something I had no time to decide.

'Now off you go collecting wood, you two!' Aunt Leonora said. 'Nice dry pieces. Ash, if possible. That burns so well.'

'I thought of helping Uncle Freddie with the rods and tackle,' I started to say.

Aunt Leonora peremptorily cut me off by brandishing the frying pan into the air.

'Oh! don't disturb the man. He likes to do it himself, in his own way.'

'Absolutely sure you don't need any help, Uncle Freddie?' I said.

Uncle Freddie, puffing with enormous contentment at his big brown pipe, merely shook his head and said 'No. Thanks all the same, dear boy.'

'There!' she said. 'I told you so. Now off you go, you and Peggy. Wooding.'

'This,' I said blandly, 'happens to be Valerie.'

'Oh! does it?' she said and gave me one of those remarkably dark accusative glares of hers, actually as if it were I who was now telling the lies.

So we went off to collect firewood, Valerie and I, walking slowly to the far end of the lake, in a morning that seemed to grow more exquisite in its summer embalmment every second. Deep woods of hazel and chestnut and alder fringed the lake on all sides and at the very far end of it a few wild duck were placidly paddling among islands of water-lilies, the new yellow buds of the flowers rising like crook-necked snakes among them. In the deepest shade of the woods,

where no sun had penetrated for weeks, a few drifts of late
bluebells still bloomed, smoky mauve.

Valerie was one of those charming animals whose presence is entirely physical. She was wearing lemon linen
shorts and an emerald nylon blouse and her legs and arms
were deeply tanned and bare. In the water she would have
been a big golden fish; on land she was more like a large,
affectionate, beautiful dog, with smooth glistening brown
hair and an occasional habit of brushing her body against
you.

'And what,' she suddenly said to me, 'was the meaning
of the big wink back there?'

I told her; I informed her, frankly, that in my opinion
my Aunt Leonora was simply doing her damnedest to fix a
match between Peggy and the undernourished Mr Benson.

'Oh! don't be silly.'

'Absolutely as plain as daylight.'

'You've got a suspicious mind.'

'Not on your life. It's an old habit of hers.'

At this she stopped on the path, in the warm sunlight now
breaking through the haze, and turned to me. She was
framed against the barely turning lower leaves of a big silver
poplar and she suddenly gave me the slowest and most
mischievous of smiles.

'You wouldn't by any chance suppose she had designs for
us too?'

'Not impossible.'

'In that case,' she said, 'aren't we going to do anything
about it?'

I murmured that I didn't see any reason at all why not
and then put my arms round her and kissed her long and
full on the mouth. The effect of this was that my body
seemed to become a 'cello on which the very deepest
reverberating notes were being played. The effect on her
was startlingly different. She finally held her big body away
from me, locking her hands softly round the nape of my
neck, and smiled full into my eyes.

'You know what?' she said. 'Kissing always makes me terribly hungry.'

'Glad to have been of service.'

'I suppose it's something to do with the mouth. But when you kissed me just now my stomach turned over and I started thinking about steak-and-kidney pie and salads and bread and cheese and custard tarts and all that sort of thing.'

'And perch.'

'Why perch?'

I briefly explained about the perch; I told her about the touch of the wild. She just laughed and said:

'Well, in that case the sooner we get back and start fishing the better.'

'You have,' I said, 'the most charming way of putting things.'

On the way back, as we gathered firewood, I couldn't help thinking that perhaps Aunt Leonora had after all made a mistake, that morning, in her careful arrangement of partners. It was really the shy Mr Benson who should have been wooding with Valerie, in the idyllic world of wild duck, yellow water-lilies and silver poplar leaves. She, undoubtedly, would have taken him clearly and finally out of himself.

But it was too late for such changes now, as I instantly discovered when we got back to where Aunt Leonora and Peggy were already laying out, in the alder shade, picnic cloth, knives and forks, pepper and salt and glasses.

In that distinctive, high-pitched voice of hers Aunt Leonora was saying:

'Never fished before? I'll bet a million to one he'll have beginner's luck. He's just that sort. He'll catch an outrageous whopper. You see.'

At these extravagant and prophetic praises of Mr Benson Peggy merely smiled shyly and polished a wine glass with a tea-cloth.

'You can feel it in some men,' Aunt Leonora said. 'Aren't you lucky?'

She could hardly have spoken with greater candour if she had suddenly speculated on the actual date of the wedding or something of that sort. She was once again at work as the great end-shaper and suddenly, almost punctually on the stroke of midday, prophecy was fulfilled. I heard a sudden excited shout from Uncle Freddie, thirty yards or so down the lake, where he and Mr Benson were already fishing.

'Hold it! Take it steady! I'll get the net!'

I promptly dropped a whole armful of wood and ran down to the lakeside. Uncle Freddie had the net in his hands and in the net was a splendid green-gold acrobatic perch, I judged of nearly a pound and a half in weight, glistening in the sun.

The expression on the pallid Mr Benson's face was one of catastrophe. It might have been the look on the face of a man who, by some ghastly mischance, has just killed a child. It was chalky with fright. His hands were trembling too and his mouth actually fell open, in an extraordinarily fish-like way, as he watched Uncle Freddie take the hook from the perch's mouth and lay the squirming fish on the grass in the sun.

'Good God!' Aunt Leonora said, rushing forward and peering excitedly through her flashing spectacles. 'What a beauty. There! Didn't I tell you?'

These last words were addressed to Peggy, who had crept up behind us with the reticence of someone coming to peer at a graveside. Her shyness was now composed completely of disbelief, which Aunt Leonora instantly shattered with another triumphant burst of candour:

'It's quite obvious you two will never starve!'

Aunt Leonora now looked almost ready to embrace Mr Benson; he might have been on the verge of entering the bosom of the family. Like a shy hero he stood watching Uncle Freddie putting another gluey pink worm on the hook and heard Valerie add still further to his discomfiture by saying, with a luscious laugh:

'My, my, a positive Isaac Walton.'

Peggy blushed deeply and with unconcealed pain. Uncle Freddie, for once really excited, declared that perch, once they got started, were great feeders. Mr Benson must therefore get at 'em; we must all get at 'em; in no time at all we'd be pulling them out by the score.

'*Filets de perche!*' Aunt Leonora exclaimed. 'Thank God I brought plenty of black pepper and butter.'

Uncle Freddie, Mr Benson and I now began feverishly to fish and soon Mr Benson, blessed by that uncanny luck that so often falls on the shoulders of beginners, was pulling out perch at the rate of one every four minutes or so. Each time he hooked a fresh one the thrill of fright went through him again, completely draining his face of blood.

Soon wood smoke was blowing fragrantly on the air.

'Somebody start bringing the fish so that I can scale and fillet them,' Aunt Leonora called. 'How many now?'

I started off towards the fire, carrying half a dozen fairsized perch in Uncle Freddie's creel. The lunch cloth was now spread out, filled with good things. Like a goldenbrown crown, the steak-and-kidney pie, in a big round baking dish, sat in the centre of an array of salads, tomatoes, radishes, brown and white loaves, cheese, custard tarts and fresh strawberries and cream.

Every now and then Aunt Leonora peered excitedly at the fish, pointedly asking to know what lucky, clever man had caught them all?

'Mr Benson,' I said. 'Uncle Freddie and I haven't had a touch.'

'What a man! What a wizard!'

After this fulsome burst of praise for Mr Benson she turned on me with one of those accusatory thrusts of hers and said she didn't suppose she could rely on me to gut and fillet the fish? I said no, indeed, she couldn't.

'If you want anything doing do it yourself,' she said. 'It's extraordinary what hidden talents *some* men have.'

I murmured that this equally applied to some women too.

'Eh? What was that?' she said. 'Mumbling again. Get

me some water. There's a washing-up bowl somewhere.'

I picked up a white enamel bowl and went down to the lake's edge to dip water. A young green frog jumped out of a bed of reeds as I filled the bowl and fell into the lake with the merest whisper of a plop. I watched it swim away and then walked back to the picnic fire just in time to hear Aunt Leonora say:

'Uncle Freddie was another dark horse. You'd never think he had it in him.'

This blatant piece of observation wasn't exactly a lie; it was just plain outrage. What was worse, she said it with an almost innocent lack of shame. It was exactly as if she were now trying to present Mr Benson not merely as the great angler but as the potential great lover, a Casanova, or something of that sort.

It was small wonder Valerie winked at me. This time I didn't wink back. Instead I was taken completely by surprise by seeing Aunt Leonora suddenly split a perch up the belly with all the deftness of an extremely practised fishmonger. A moment later a cloud of blood filled the bowl and for a moment I thought Peggy would be sick.

By now the morning was growing hot and it seemed to me an appropriate moment to test the temperature of the red-currant wine. I went to fetch a bottle from the lake. It was already beautifully cool but Aunt Leonora looked at it with a glare of dark disapprobation.

'And who gave you permission to start on the wine?'

'Uncle Freddie.'

'Don't fib.'

I said I liked this. And added: 'You, I suppose, don't want any?'

'Good grief, man, don't be dim. And you'd better take a glass to Mr Benson. *He* certainly deserves it.'

The two girls, I noticed, had retreated for a walk. Blood, scales, fins, tails and fish-guts were strewn everywhere. A strange, half-muddy, half-fishy odour hung on the air. I felt my appetite start to drift away.

Farther down the lake Mr Benson's luck, perhaps happily, had started to wane. He too was hot. Sweat was pouring from his brow and nose. Uncle Freddie greeted the sight of the wine with cries of relish and an enthusiastic: 'Splendid thought, dear boy. Bless you. Absolute salvation.'

Parched with excitement and thirst, Mr Benson sat on the bank and drank the wine in deep draughts, as if it had been mere rose-coloured water.

'Any more fish?' I said.

Uncle Freddie said only two and not very large at that. They seemed, he thought, to be suddenly off feed. I said I would take them and a moment later started to carry away, in the keep-net, the brace of perch, not much more than tiddlers: so small indeed that half-way to the camp fire, as much out of selfish regard for my appetite as a sense of pity, I dropped them quietly back into the lake.

Gold spectacles dancing, her hands bloody as if from some messy sacrifice, Aunt Leonora demanded to know how the miraculous Mr Benson was faring now? His luck, I told her, had left him; the fish were suddenly off feed. This information, far from lowering Mr Benson in her eyes, merely seemed to elevate him further and she gave a half-ecstatic gasp and said:

'He's been marvellous. He's saved the morning. Isn't she lucky?'

'Isn't who lucky?'

'That girl. Valerie.'

'Good God, not Valerie. Anyway here they are coming back. For Heaven's sake take a good look at them. Valerie's the big golden one – '

She wasn't listening. Instead she was washing her hands of blood. When they were dry and clean again she laid a number of perch fillets, I think twelve or fourteen of them, side by side in the frying pan. They were a queer greenish mud colour, not at all unlike the colour of the frog I had seen jump into the lake, but she dabbed lavish lumps of butter all over them with something like reverent rapture.

'Put more sticks on the fire. And where is the wine for Heaven's sake? I suppose you men have been fairly slopping it down.'

I put more wood on the fire; I said I would go to fetch the wine; and as I walked away I heard her call in shrill double command:

'Girls! Start cutting bread. And call Uncle Freddie and dear Mr Benson. They've five minutes to get their hands washed. I'm cooking.'

When I got back from fetching the wine and instructing Uncle Freddie and Mr Benson to get ready for lunch the strangest of odours filled the air. It floated everywhere with a sickly twang, a noisome compound of wood smoke, burning butter, drying mud and a fishmonger's back-yard on a hot afternoon. There was also a monstrous sizzling to be heard as Aunt Leonora poked and turned the fish with an egg-slice.

Valerie, I noticed, was vigorously making up her face and heavily spattering her bosom with perfume, but whatever scent she was using faded on the air like a delicate moth against a powerful flight of hornets. By contrast Peggy seemed shyer, quieter than ever and, I thought, awfully, ominously pale.

Some minutes later Mr Benson and Uncle Freddie came slowly up the lake path, each carrying two bottles of wine. Ten yards from the fire Uncle Freddie suddenly stopped dead, said 'Good God' in an alarmingly loud voice and recoiled a good two feet from the pan of perch.

'And what are you good-Godding about? You've washed your hands I hope? Sit yourselves down – we're nearly ready.'

'I mean it's awfully hot – I mean the fire – '

'Mr Benson, sit yourself next to Valerie. You,' she said to me, 'start pouring the wine. Don't slack about so!'

If I had any idea of doing anything about this shrill rebuke I was saved from the necessity of it by Uncle Freddie. With hands positively tottering and with the eagerness of a traveller at the end of some parching desert trek he was already pouring a large measure of wine for Mr Benson and an even larger one for himself.

Mr Benson, I noticed, was ominously flushed. His normally pallid face was wreathed in a tipsy pinkish cloud. Aunt Leonora's notions of taking him out of himself had succeeded so well indeed that he now seemed almost a stranger. His eyes had in them a moist groping glow and suddenly I saw him turn them on Peggy in a second of fleeting, helpless appeal. She for her part could do nothing but appeal as mutely in return.

In the smoky heat of that fishy, sombre midday, Aunt Leonora suddenly gave a girlish shriek, said 'Ready!', brandished the sizzling frying pan and commanded all of us to sit down and fall to.

For one awful moment I thought Mr Benson would fall. His legs seemed momentarily to totter under him. He ended by flopping heavily between Valerie and Peggy, most of his wine spilling on the way.

All the time that monstrous canopy of muddy fishiness hung over us. And soon the fish itself was on our plates, greenish, gluey, glassy with hot butter. Then as we began to toy with it, some of us with politeness, some not, and most of us under heavy cover of bread, Aunt Leonora suddenly glared across at me from behind her dancing gold spectacles and demanded to know:

'Well, how does it strike you?'

In a low voice, from behind a hunk of bread, I simply said that it struck me.

'Eh? What was that?' Those charming big teeth of hers almost snapped at me. 'Don't mutter. I've told you before.'

'Oh! the fish?' I said. 'Quite indescribable.'

'What? How do you mean? Indescribable?'

'Just indescribable.'

She gave me one of those dark searching glowers of hers, at the same time masticating with blatant richness on a lump of perch, and then said:

'Well, I won't claim they have quite the *finesse* of those we had at Geneva – the waters are colder there anyway and that makes a difference – but I've had worse. I've had worse.'

I was about to ask where? when she peremptorily accused Uncle Freddie of neglecting the wine.

'Mr Benson's glass is empty, isn't it, Mr Benson? Disgraceful. If any man's glass should be full it's Mr Benson's. Fill the dear man to the brim.'

Mr Benson, who was in no position to know whether his glass was full or empty, gave a slight retching sound but otherwise made no reply. At the same time Uncle Freddie took an enormous swig of wine, gulped at some impossible lump of fish stuck in his throat, smacked his lips, and involuntarily belched aloud.

'Freddie!'

Peggy coughed weakly on a fish-bone. I hadn't the heart to look at Valerie, nor she at me, but suddenly I felt the air to be full of desperation.

'Oh! look at the swans, Aunt. And five cygnets.'

She turned sharply to look at the lake.

'Swans? What swans? Where? I don't see swans.'

'Over there. No – not that way – farther up. By the island. You see the quince trees? Just beyond. You mustn't miss them – they look like a bit of ballet.'

Her nature, as well as being that of a schemer, is also an intensely curious one and she abruptly got up and walked over to the lake.

In the interval of her being there I threw two buttery fillets over my shoulder, into a clump of cow parsley. Uncle Freddie solemnly wrapped two of his in a handkerchief. I saw Valerie slide one of hers under the table-cloth and for the second time within a few minutes drench her beautiful breast in perfume. She also winked at me and I, prompted by this, wrapped the remains of Peggy's perch in a paper napkin. In return she had neither wink nor smile for me but nstead was gazing at Mr Benson with a kind of remote and pained compassion. There were almost tears in her eyes.

'What swans? You must be imagining things. I could see no swans.'

'You were too late.'

Before she could counter this Mr Benson staggered slowly to his feet.

'Would you mind,' he said, 'if I just went for a little walk?'

Flushed and tottering, he started to grope his way along the lakeside. He had scarcely gone twenty yards or so before Aunt Leonora, with that smile of divine triumph of hers, leaned over to Peggy, touched her lightly on the hand and said in a breath of almost secretive sweetness:

'Go with him, dear. I think he needs your help.'

As Peggy got up to go I could hear Mr Benson being horribly sick by the lakeside. At the first ghastly groan of his pain she broke into a cry and started running and for the rest of that sombre humid afternoon she sat under the shadow of a silver poplar, Mr Benson's head in her lap, just occasionally shyly stroking his hair. And occasionally also, as Aunt Leonora looked with fond solicitude on the two of them, Aunt Leonora would give that charming, innocent toothy smile of hers and say something like:

'You think they're all right? They've had no food. You think we should take them a piece of pie? Perhaps not. Perhaps they're best left together. When two people are together like that I don't suppose they're interested in food. No, let's leave them. Perhaps they'll have a zizz. Then they can have pie when they wake up. I thought the crust was so good today.'

This triumph of divine end-shaping happened a long time ago. Mr Benson and Peggy are married now and once a year, on their wedding anniversary, Aunt Leonora always gives them a little dinner party, to which I too am invited. Always we drink red-currant wine and always, with that divine tactlessness of hers which so infuriates and fascinates, she serves one course of fish fried in butter. And always, half way through this course, I look up first at Peggy and then at Mr Benson and see on their two faces the same strange, lost, distant, groping look.

It is exactly as if they had never met each other before.

The Old Eternal

EVERY year the elderly Miss Rigby and the slightly older Miss Pinkerton, affectionately known to each other as Spud and Pinkie, celebrated some part of Christmas by having a few glasses of port, a slice of plum cake and a wedge of Cheshire cheese in the old air-raid shelter that still stood, after so many years, under their bottom garden wall.

'Sort of thanksgiving for what we got through at the time,' they would explain.

Late in the autumn, after the leaves of the pumpkins that always grew on the roof of the shelter had been blackened to sloppy pulp by the first frosts, Pinkie raked off the old dead vines, scrubbed down the interior corrugated iron with strong carbolic soap and opened the door for several days to give the shelter what she called 'a bit of a sweetener'.

Pinkie was small, very cherubic and fierily red in the face, with light blue eyes that protruded eagerly like little silver thimbles. After a few drops of what she called 'the you know what' she glowed hotly, with positively mustard-like excitement, and chattered with panting merriment, looking like a breathless Pekinese. In the household she rushed from object to object in sniffing and palpitating pursuit, as if everywhere seeking a hidden bone.

Miss Rigby, Spud, was neither so active nor so lucky. She was big, slow, imperturbable and misshapen. Her face was so like a large discoloured potato that the name Spud really suited her. She suffered, among other things, from painful swellings of the legs, uneasy shortness of breath and false teeth that didn't fit very well and continually got gummed together by pieces of marshmallow, her favourite sweetmeat. But these minor pains never discouraged her. She waddled everywhere with wheezy and jovial optimism, sometimes carrying large orange pumpkins about, nursing them in her arms like fat babies to which she had miraculously given birth.

In the shelter all the antique paraphernalia of war-time – the war was so far away and yet sometimes seemed like only yesterday – was preserved as it had always been: stirrup pump and two buckets, one of water and one of sand, torch, candle in its holder, whistle and even a pair of gas-masks neatly hung in their khaki bags on the wall.

A small square window, its glass of the kind that is reinforced with wire, gave out on to the garden, and here Spud and Pinkie sat on the afternoon of Christmas Eve, gazing at the damp earth outside, sipping port-wine and munching on cake and cheese.

'We always seem to have good weather,' Pinkie said. 'Goodness knows what we'd do if it snowed.'

'Of course you know what we'd do if it snowed,' Spud said. 'We'd sit here just the same. It would take more than that to put us off.'

'I suppose so. I suppose so. I suppose it would, Spud dear.'

'Do you remember how it snowed in 1940?' Spud said. 'We got snowed in and there were enormous drifts and we couldn't get out again.'

They laughed in chorus at this: Spud rather like a deep French horn, Pinkie like a cymbal.

'And I blew so hard on the whistle to get Mr Ackerly to come and dig us out I thought I'd blow my teeth out,' Spud said. 'I always say that's what first loosened them.'

They laughed again at this and Pinkie poured more port. It didn't seem like Christmas until they were well on with the port and they could hear the evening bells across the town. The candle always made a difference too and presently Spud said:

'Let's have the candle alight, shall we, Pinkie? I love the glow of the port in the candlelight.'

'I'll do it, Spud dear, I'll do it. Don't move.'

In the candlelight it was not only the port that glowed.

Pinkie glowed too, a fiery little cherub flashing silver thimble-eyes.

'Funny how the candle all of a sudden makes it seem dark outside,' she said. 'And then you see that wonderful blue in the sky. And the first stars.'

'They say the band will be coming this way on Christmas Eve this year,' Spud said, 'instead of Christmas morning.'

'Oh! do they? I didn't put their Christmas-box ready. You think I ought to pop back and get it in case they arrive?'

'No, no. Sit still. We shall hear them when they come.'

'You mean we will if we don't drop off. You remember the year we both dropped off? And slept through that awful raid? Sound as babies. And everybody said how ghastly it was.'

They laughed again at this stirring and hilarious memory and Pinkie poured out a further drop of port. War was awfully funny, really, depending on how you looked at it.

'I don't see it starting to rain, do I?' Pinkie huffed on the little glass window and then rubbed it with the sleeve of her musquash coat and peered out. 'No, I don't think so.' She champed on a piece of plum cake like an eager puppy. 'I tell you what I do see. though. There's somebody in the garden. Wandering around.'

'Not the Angel Gabriel, is it?' Spud said. 'We don't want him here. Not yet, anyway.'

This was the signal for another jovial duet of laughter and then Pinkie opened the door of the shelter and called:

'Hullo there. Who is it? Who's about?'

An answering voice called 'Hullo there!' and Pinkie said:

'Oh! it's you, Mr Ackerly. We're in here. In the shelter.'

'What's come over him?' Spud said. 'He doesn't usually call till Christmas Day. Everybody's changing their habits.'

'Come in, Mr Ackerly, if you can get in,' Pinkie said. 'Come and join us.'

'Yes,' Spud said, 'come and join our happy throng.'

Mr Ackerly, a tall stooping figure looking rather like

a pessimistic giraffe with a bowler hat on, appeared from the outer gloom, carrying a bottle wrapped in tissue paper.

'What a nice surprise,' Spud said. 'What brings you on Christmas Eve? You usually come tomorrow.'

'Oh! I don't know.' Pessimism oozed out of Mr Ackerly like dark vapour; there was almost a cloud about the candle. 'After all, there might not *be* a tomorrow.'

'Now don't start talking about The Bomb again,' Spud said. 'It's Christmas Eve.'

'No, no, not The Bomb, please,' Pinkie said. 'Have a drop of port. I'll go and get another glass for you.'

'Oh! I don't know if I should – '

'Oh! of course you should!' Spud said. 'Sit down. I don't like you standing up. You're so tall I feel you'll lift our dear old shelter off its feet.'

While Pinkie raced puppy-like across the garden to get another glass from the house, Mr Ackerly sat down and stared about him with increasing gloom. Our dear old shelter – did you ever hear anything like it? Heavens, it was awful. Whatever made them do it every year? Dear old shelter – there was a terrible monkish sort of odour about the place that repelled him. The mould of death lay on it – it really made him shudder.

Candlelight always depressed him too, anyway. What with that and The Bomb it seemed a pretty desolate outlook, he thought, as he sat there staring at Spud, the trembling candle and all the silly, derelict paraphernalia of wartime. He couldn't for the life of him fathom what made them do it. The future was bleak enough without dragging up the past.

Cheerfully, actually humming a few bars of *Christians Awake!*, Pinkie came back from the house with a glass for Mr Ackerly.

'Just a modicum,' Mr Ackerly said. 'That's ample – '

The sight of Pinkie pouring the port reminded Mr Ackerly that he was the bearer of a gift. With a struggling sigh he handed over the bottle to Spud as if it were The Bomb itself.

'Just my usual little offering to both of you.' He seemed to be about to render the first notes of a sepulchral anthem.

'You'd better drink it up quick. If you ask me we haven't got much time.'

Pinkie shut the door of the shelter and Spud ripped off the tissue wrapping of the bottle as if it concealed a new hat.

'Oh! our favourite whisky. Nice man. Thank you so awfully much,' Spud said. 'Kiss.'

Mr Ackerly, with despondent reluctance, suffered himself to be kissed first on one cheek by Spud and then on the other by Pinkie.

'How nice. How generous of you. Well, cheers,' Spud said. 'Here's to Christmas. And the best of luck in the future.'

'Great Heavens, we'll need it,' Mr Ackerly said. 'No, we won't though, because there isn't going to be any.'

'Any what?' Spud said. 'Future? Don't talk out of your back collar-stud, man.'

'Everybody was saying that in 1940,' Pinkie said. 'And dear knows they were the dark days – '

'Ah!' Mr Ackerly said, 'but this is different. This is different.'

Spud laughed again, French-horn fashion, and held out her glass.

'I'll have a drop more, Pinkie dear, please. I need fortifying.'

'We all do,' Mr Ackerly said. 'That's why I say "Drink up your bottle while you can." There isn't much time. There can't be.'

'I vote we do that,' Spud said. 'What say, Pinkie? I feel in that mood.'

'You know me,' Pinkie said. 'I'm game for anything. Especially the you know what. It's Christmas anyway.'

Again the duet of careless laughter, to Mr Ackerly's increasing despondency, echoed merrily about the shelter.

Where, he thought, was there any possible cause for laughter? The terrible dark claw of everlasting oblivion was hanging over all of them and the best these two could do was howl with laughter. You might have thought it was just some silly bun fight.

'Shall we start the whisky?' Spud said. 'Let's.'

She drained her third glass of port, at the same time urging Mr Ackerly to drink up, and held out her empty glass to Pinkie, who immediately started to tot out whisky.

'Oh! by the way,' Pinkie said. 'Don't let me forget when you go. We've got the most marvellous pumpkin chutney for you.'

Pumpkin chutney! – Mr Ackerly was shocked to speechlessness. Pumpkin chutney! – Ye Gods, it was as if in the middle of a terrible and obliterating earthquake you sat trying to thread a needle. It was like sitting under the fiery lava of Vesuvius trying to set a mouse trap.

When he had partly recovered from the ghastly incongruity of the whole thing he started to get up and say:

'If you don't mind I think I ought to be getting along.'

'Oh! no you don't,' Spud said. 'You're going to have some whisky. After all it was your idea.'

'Of course,' Pinkie said. 'Don't be inconsistent.'

'No, but really I ought to go. It's getting dark and I've quite a lot –'

'Dark?' Spud said. 'Good Heavens, man, you're not frightened, are you?'

'No, no,' Mr Ackerly said. 'I'm not frightened of *anything*.'

'Do have some whisky,' Pinkie said. She sat sipping at her glass, all rosy fire in the candlelight, occasionally smacking her lips exactly like a panting little dog. 'It's delicious.'

'Do you mind if I don't mix it?' Mr Ackerly said. 'It really isn't good for me.'

'Have a piece of plum cake and some cheese,' Spud said. 'They go awfully well together.'

With rising nausea Mr Ackerly rejected the idea of cake

and cheese and then slowly sat down again, painfully resigned.

'We got quite tight once,' Pinkie said, 'didn't we, Spud dear?'

'Gloriously.'

Appropriately glorious peals of laughter greeted this new memory, filling Mr Ackerly with a fresh amazement.

'And when we woke,' Spud said, 'the Ritz cinema had gone. Half of Cromwell Street and Johnson's factory had gone. And the Baptist chapel and half the railway works. And we never knew a thing. The stars must have been watching over us that night.'

Mr Ackerly could think of no coherent or sensible answer to this reminiscence, which was offered as if it were a scene from some reckless pantomime. Again the shelter rang with laughter.

'Do I hear the band?' Pinkie said. 'I think I do.'

A hush fell on the shelter. Pinkie opened the door and leaned out, poised and alert as a setter, listening.

'All the stars are shining,' she said, 'and yes, it's the band.'

'Leave the door open,' Spud said, 'I like to hear it.'

It was chilly with the door open. A sharp draught swept about Mr Ackerly's feet and legs. He was going to catch his death of cold; he knew he would.

'They were playing *Oh! Come All Ye Faithful*,' Pinkie said. 'They've stopped now.'

'Means they're on their way here, I suppose,' Spud said. 'I think you ought to go and get the Christmas Box ready now, Pinkie dear.'

'I think so too. How much? Five shillings?'

'Oh! ten. After all it's only Christmas once a year.'

Pinkie fled across the darkened garden, leaving Spud sipping with cushiony content at her whisky and Mr Ackerly bowed under deeper vapours of gloom. There would, he told himself, be no more Christmasses. Let there be no illusion about that. This, he thought, was the last there would ever be.

He was about to express these profoundly despondent thoughts to Spud when, outside in the street, the band struck up, brassily playing *It Came Upon the Midnight Clear*. Spud drank and listened. She wouldn't be hearing that tune many more times, Mr Ackerly assured her miserably, but Spud didn't seem to listen and didn't seem to care. Under the influence of port and whisky she had suddenly begun to feel merriment drive out contentment and now and then she gave a fruity chuckle.

'How you can sit there chuckling in what is probably the most solemn and awful crisis in all history I cannot think,' Mr Ackerly said. 'It's dreadful – it's wicked, it's tempting Providence.'

'I was thinking of one of the men who plays the euphonium in the band,' Spud said. 'Fred Sanders. He's so small. He isn't much bigger than the euphonium. He taught Pinkie to blow last year. Just one note, mind you.'

'I can't say I know him.'

'I love him,' Spud said, taking a big plum out of a piece of cake and gazing at it lovingly. 'He's great fun.'

Suddenly she gave up gazing at the plum and popped it in her mouth and then, thinking that she saw Pinkie moving in the light of the house, wobbled to the doorway of the shelter and called:

'Is that you, Pinkie dear? Who's collecting tonight? Fred?'

Pinkie's merrily twittering voice called back that she didn't know and they'd only played one carol yet and she thought that really, for ten bob, they ought to have two.

'Well, find Fred anyway and bring him over for a tot.'

While waiting for Pinkie to come back Spud insisted on Mr Ackerly having another drop of port. This time he was too depressed to refuse and anyway he simply had to do something to keep out that dreadful cold. What a ghastly mocking situation it was to be sitting there under the Shadow of The Bomb and perhaps, all the time, simply catching your death of cold in the ordinary way. It hardly bore thinking about. You hadn't a ghost of a chance whichever way you looked at it.

Meanwhile the band played *Silent Night, Holy Night* and the melancholy beauty of the tune suddenly drove Mr Ackerly to the verge of tears. He had the greatest difficulty in stifling a sob and in order to do so drank half a glass of port very quickly, gulping loudly.

Spud took the opportunity to top up his glass and a moment later Pinkie was back, bringing Fred Sanders, who in turn had brought his euphonium. Fred was dressed in a maroon-coloured bandsman's uniform with gold frogs and epaulettes and a matching peaked cap with the words *Temperance Silver Band* ringed across it.

'So very nice to see you, Fred. Happy Christmas! Port or whisky?'

'Well, I've been on whisky,' Fred said, 'except for a couple of beers before we started.'

'Whisky it had better be,' Spud said. 'Come into the office anyway.'

Fred, who propped up his euphonium by the door, had a way of laughing that was discordant but not unpleasant, rather like one of those tunes played on an old cracked piano. His voice suddenly inspired both Pinkie and Spud to fresh merriment and they blessed him with: 'Cheers and a happy Christmas and many of them.'

'Mr Ackerly here thinks this'll be the last one we'll ever have,' Spud said.

'Gorblimey, why?'

'The Bomb.'

'Oh! to ruddy 'ell with The Bomb,' Fred said. 'Stone the crows.'

'You hear what Fred says?' Spud asked Mr Ackerly. 'To ruddy Hell with The Bomb and stone the crows.'

'Stoning the crows isn't the sort of expedient I should recommend in this crisis,' Mr Ackerly said. 'Don't you *see?* – we're *doomed!*'

'No?' Fred said. 'Well, you're only dead once.'

'That's true,' Pinkie said, laughing lightly. She was beginning to feel a higher sense of merriment too. Again she laughed, this time with little shrieks, and suddenly said she wondered if Fred was going to give them a little tune on the euphonium. Like he did last year. 'Do Fred, please.'

'I might if I get another wet,' Fred said, and let off a few of his own cracked scales of laughter.

'That's right, let's all have another wet,' Spud said. 'Mr Ackerly, what about another drop of Strontium Ninety – ?'

Spud, Pinkie and Fred roared with laughter but the mention of Strontium Ninety under conditions that would have been farcical if they had not been tragic seemed to Mr Ackerly a terrible and shocking heresy. He could neither speak nor drink. The port filled him with revulsion and suddenly he felt the draught from the door climb up his spine like a chilling long-legged spider.

Fred, who hadn't much idea what Strontium Ninety was, watched his glass being filled by Pinkie with eager relish. He quickly knocked back his whisky, gave another cracked laugh and then asked what would it be? The tune, he meant.

'*Nearer my God to Thee*, Mr Ackerly?'

'Oh! please. Don't joke. Please.'

'Play what you played for us last year,' Pinkie said. 'You said it was your favourite one.'

'But that ain't a carol,' Fred said.

'I know it isn't. But I like it all the same. It puts you in such good humour.'

'*Little Brown Jug*, wasn't it?' Spud said. 'Yes, I remember now.'

To play *Little Brown Jug* while the Shadow of The Bomb was hanging over them seemed to Mr Ackerly an even more shocking heresy than talking of drinking Strontium Ninety in an old air-raid shelter, but as the ghastly noise of the euphonium rang through the shelter he was equally shocked to see both Spud and Pinkie singing loudly and then soon, hand in hand, dancing round.

'My wife and I lived all alone
In a little log hut we called our own.
She loved gin and I loved rum –
I tell you what, we'd lots of fun.
Ha, ha, ha! you and me,
Little Brown jug don't I love thee!'

they sang; and then suddenly Spud shouted:

'Happy Christmas to everybody! Let 'em all come! And to ruddy Hell with The Bomb!'

'To blazes with it!' Pinkie said. 'And stone the crows.'

'Are we down-'earted?' Fred suddenly asked and got from the ladies an almost thunderous answer:

'No! !'

Only Mr Ackerly was down-hearted. The strident noise of the euphonium and the singing were altogether too much for him and he now sought refuge in the garden, shivering.

'What about me blowing a note now, Fred?' Pinkie said. 'Like last year.'

'That's a good idea,' Fred said. 'Blow the old raspberry.'

'Splendid,' Spud said. 'Splendid. Let's all go outside.'

In the garden Pinkie embraced the euphonium with fond anticipation, pointing the horn to the sky. She had almost forgotten which of the valves to press but Fred soon put her right on this and then urged her:

'Go on. Now give 'er all you got, Miss. Ready? – one, two, three! – '

Pinkie blew hard, instantly producing what Fred called 'a bit of a rag-tearer', a rude single blast that rose on the night air with something like defiance, mocking the darkness.

'Splendid!' Spud said. 'Old Gabriel couldn't have done better. What price our new bandsman, Mr Ackerly?'

'Mr Ackerly's gone,' Fred said. 'You blowed 'im to Kingdom come.'

'Oh dear, the poor man's gone and forgotten his pumpkin chutney,' Pinkie said.

Mr Ackerly's sudden, silent departure was a signal for not

only another merry trio of laughter but in due course another whisky for Fred. As he prepared to drink it he wished the ladies 'A very happy Christmas and many of 'em' and they wished him the same in return. They also kissed him on both cheeks, Pinkie so enthusiastically that his bandsman's cap was knocked askew, with the result that the words *Temperance Silver Band* were very much to one side.

'Well, no use, I must be going,' Fred said. 'Never catch 'em up – '

'Good-bye, Fred. Lovely seeing you. Happy, happy Christmas.'

'Good-bye, Fred,' Pinkie said. 'And what do we say?'

'Let 'em all come!' Fred said. 'That's what we say!'

Like a silver ghost the euphonium passed across the garden. When it had disappeared into darkness Pinkie and Spud stood for some time framed in the door-way of the shelter, silent in the candlelight, looking up at the sky.

The laughter was over now.

'Shall we thank our lucky stars, Pinkie dear? We always do.'

In silence they held up their glasses to the stars.

'They always look so awfully eternal somehow, don't they, Spud dear?'

By this time the band was playing again, now further away, and the sound of bells was bright across the town.

'That's the way they always look to me,' Spud said. 'But then I like to think we're a bit of the old eternal too.'

Captain Poop-Deck's Paradise

It was while walking home from an afternoon's dull and desultory pike-fishing that I met Captain Poop-Deck for the first and only time. My pet name for him fitted him rather well, I thought.

The day was one of those airless, humid ones in late August that seem to sap the energy of both man and fish alike and when even the leaves of poplars hardly turn in the air.

The weather, however, was having no such effect on Captain Poop-Deck, who was briskly and merrily rubbing down the old brown paint of a shabby fifty-foot cabin cruiser chocked up on a grey stretch of gravel beside a thick wood of alder trees. Two young, smart, well-built girls were helping him, both with big pots of white paint, one of them actually hanging over the port side of the boat on a cradle, her large haunches bulging like magenta linen footballs. The other was a splendid fleshy girl of twenty or so dressed in navy blue shorts and a very nautical blue-and-white striped shirt and a yachting cap from under which her dark hair hung down in a single pig-tail over her left shoulder.

Captain Poop-Deck, who looked about sixty, was also wearing a yachting cap, well cocked to one side, and it wouldn't have surprised me very much if he too had sported a pig-tail. He looked altogether not unlike a very handsome pirate left over from a fancy dress ball. His frame was extraordinarily big-boned and muscular and was draped – dressed would be far too formal a word – in a thick scarlet flannel shirt, canary yellow trousers held up by a brass belt fastened with a snake buckle and bright blue straw shoes. Round his neck he was wearing a stiff black and white scarf tied in such a way as to give more or less the effect of skull and cross-bones and as he rubbed at the paint he sang in sudden heaving crescendo of wordless song.

Seeing me pass with my rods and perhaps even guessing that I was cursing a certain luckless dejection he cheerily waved a strip of sand-paper in my direction and called:

'Hail there! Any luck, sir?'

His voice, for so large a man, was smooth and soft as oil. It was quite cultivated too.

'No,' I had to confess, 'not a touch. Too warm, I suppose.'

'After chub?'

'No,' I told him, 'pike.'

'The chub are the boys here,' he said. 'Feller here last Sunday had a seven-pounder. And then, damme, about a quarter of an hour later, whipped out a twelve-pounder. Looked as big as a shark.'

I stared Captain Poop-Deck very firmly in the eye. He didn't flinch a bit and the big transparent blue circles blandly placed between the sauciness of the yachting cap and the flamboyance of the skull and cross-bones might have been the eyes of a trusting child.

'Come aboard, sir, and look the ship over,' he suddenly said. 'Come and have a noggin. We opened a keg at lunch-time.'

I was tired; I was very thirsty; and I wanted to get home.

'The beer keeps ice-cold below decks or Lola'll mix us a planter's punch, won't you, Bo'sun?'

Lola was the girl with the magenta footballs; she was as blonde as thistledown and she turned and gave me a slow, flowery smile.

'The bo'sun mixes a beauty,' Captain Poop-Deck said. 'Heave yourself aboard, sir.'

Half a minute later I was heaving myself up a rope-ladder that looked about as trustworthy as a string bag and Poop-Deck was pulling me aboard with a warm and ebullient hand.

'Welcome aboard, sir. Splendid to know you. Meet my first mate,' he said. 'Tina.' The girl with the pig-tail gave me a quick, snappy smile. 'Best Number One who ever sailed.'

At that moment it crossed my mind that she was exactly the sort of girl men dream of being wrecked on desert islands with; at the same time I was unaware of how near the truth I was until suddenly I looked towards the stern end of the boat and saw there a quite remarkable flag.

It was of bright scarlet, with a brilliant canary yellow coconut palm worked across the middle. The colours so resembled those of the Captain's shirt and trousers that the flag might well have been made from bits of the same material left over.

'Ah! I see you're admiring our flag,' the Captain said.

'It's very unusual. Why the palm tree?'

'It's the flag of our expedition.'

'Expedition?'

'We sail for tropic waters as soon as we're ship-shape. Didn't you read about it in the press a couple of weeks ago? Splendid write-up.'

With the deftness of a life-long conjurer Poop-Deck whipped from his shirt pocket a long press-cutting in which a picture of himself dominated everything like that of an uncrowned king.

'Peruse that. Sit yourself down. The bosun'll be here any moment now with the grog.'

I had hardly time to catch a glimpse of the words 'South Sea Adventure. Former Naval Officer Promises Other Eden', before the Captain squatted down on the deck and said:

'Brought me over a hundred replies in no time. People clamouring, fighting to join us. True, Number One? Without the word of a lie? Sit yourself down,' he said again. 'Sit yourself down.'

With trepidation I sat on an empty beer-barrel. I had the

sudden feeling that the deck of the boat was rather like an old ship's biscuit; at any moment it might crumble away.

'And still they come. Every day. How many today, Number One?'

'Nine.'

'Nine more today, sir. And seven, I think, yesterday.'

By now a few doubts had begun to enter my mind. Once again I stared Captain Poop-Deck straight in the eye and once again there was no hint of flinching. The blandness of his eyes even succeeded in making me feel slightly embarrassed at having had the presumption to doubt him and I almost wished I hadn't started to say:

'But this boat would never take a hundred people.'

'Naturally not. Naturally not. But they can all participate equally as bond-holders in the scheme.'

I didn't much care for the word 'participate' or for 'bond-holders' either and I was glad to look up and see the bo'sun coming up from below decks with the grog: four handsome rum punches in long glasses each richly topped with nuts, mint-sprigs and straws.

As I took my glass I started to say something about the drinks reminding me of Jamaica but the Captain cut me short with the friendliest enthusiasm:

'Ah! then, you know the tropics, sir?'

'Slightly. Where exactly are you bound for?'

The Captain looked secretive, in a way almost coy. By now the two girls were squatting on the deck too, looking rather like two worshipful hand-maidens awaiting the pleasure of their master.

'Sealed orders,' the Captain said. 'Daren't say a word. Place would be swarming with tricksters in no time. No: all I can say is that I've had the great good fortune to come into possession of this island. And not being a selfish man I want to share it with others.'

'Desert island of course?'

'Not precisely. Not precisely. There is habitation. There

used to be a sugar factory but that's gone now. Bags of water. Wild donkeys – which we shall tame and use of course – and plenty of bird-life, game and so forth.'

'And palms,' the bo'sun said, taking the straw from her mouth, almost coyly too. 'Don't forget the palms.'

'Clever girl, the bo'sun. Always remembers the important things. Palms, of course, palms. The emblem of the expedition. As witness our flag.'

'The palms are important, are they?' I said.

'Nothing more so. The coconut palm is man's best friend. Forget about the dog. It's the coconut palm. Where the coconut palm grows man can never starve. The meat and milk of the coconut will feed him. The tree will build his house and give him a roof for his head. How do you think the Polynesians survived on those long world-voyages of theirs? On floating coconuts. Nuts drifting on the great South Pacific currents gave them their milk and meat. For months. For years.'

'You've been there, of course?'

The Captain, after silently sipping at his straw for some moments, eyes down, at last looked up at me with an expression almost pained.

'Everyone asks that question. I wonder why. The fact that you've never been to a place doesn't mean it's not there. You've never been to the South Pole but it's there. Nobody has yet been to the moon but it's there. I haven't yet been to my island but it's there.'

As the Captain expounded this beautiful piece of logic the bo'sun and the first mate sat looking at him with complete entrancement, almost rapture, and the bosom of Lola, the bigger girl, several times gave a great expanding heave.

After a silence in which I too sipped at my glass – the punch was really excellent, prepared with skill and care – I suddenly remembered the Captain's words about the scheme.

'How does the scheme work?' I said.

'You mean you're thinking perhaps of participating? I don't know about that, I'm sure. We're pretty chock-a-block already. Almost embarrassing. The thing's gone like stink, I mean. Like wildfire. That's why we're working like blacks to get ship-shape. Got to sail by October.'

'Tell me about the scheme, anyway.'

Well, it worked like this, the Captain went on to say. The island was roughly twenty-five miles long and ten wide. Two hundred and fifty square miles. Ample room for two hundred and fifty people and no treading on toes. For units of twenty-five, fifty, seventy-five, one hundred or two hundred pounds – two hundred was the statutory limit, he said, and I liked very much the word statutory – a bond-holder would get a parcel of land, each parcel of land with shore frontage or access to it, of one acre, two acres, three acres and so on.

'To be his or hers,' the Captain said, 'without strings, in perpetuity, for ever. It's as simple as that. Another punch?'

I was about to decline the offer of a second punch when suddenly I changed my mind.

'Splendid,' the Captain said. 'The bo'sun will get it. And one for me too.'

I thought the bo'sun went below decks with a certain reluctance, a little unwilling to surrender her seat as hand-maiden in the sun, and after she had gone I said:

'Tell me, what about money?'

'On the island you mean?' The Captain actually laughed, his voice quite honied. 'My dear fellow, there will be no money. It isn't necessary. That's the marvellous, simple beauty of the scheme. Nothing to be bought, nothing to be sold – so why money? The palm, as I say, will house us. There's water everywhere. The place teems with grub. Yams, bread-fruit, guavas, limes, sweet potatoes, game, fish, wild pig – Good grief, my friend, we're fleeing from money, not seeking it.'

'It's an ideal that man has always pursued, of course.'

'Of course. Exactly. For centuries. For thousands of years. And what has stopped him? Greed, man, greed.'

'Exactly. By the way, how would we get there?'

'Did you say "we"?' The Captain's eyes shone not merely with embullience now but with a benevolence of truly engaging charm. 'You mean you want to be in? I had really made up my mind "No", but I rather like you. You talk sense. You're in.'

'You still haven't told me how we get there.'

'As the advance party, in this, the boat.' The Captain rapped his knuckles hard on the deck and I almost seemed to hear it splinter. '*The Other Eden.* That's her name. The first mate thought of that, didn't you, Tina? Shakespeare.'

The first mate gave the Captain a smile of pure enslavement, tossing her pig-tail rather nervously, I thought, from one shoulder to another.

'As for those who come later, they travel either by air or sea to the Cook Islands, from which we shall run a weekly ferry service by the *Eden* to the island at a purely nominal charge. By the way, it takes quite a few days to get these bonds through. They have to be very carefully drawn up and vetted and then registered in London of course.'

'Of course. No hurry.'

'Made up your mind which unit you might take up?'

'Not yet. I'll give it careful thought, though.'

The Captain seemed pleased and said he would tell me something else I might have forgotten. This was no ordinary paradise. It was the perfect refuge from that evil thing, the Bomb.

'We might, in the event, be the only people left alive on earth.'

'We might indeed.'

'That's the part that really attracts people. They're all fed to the teeth with this mad, modern set-up. They loathe the ruddy bomb, the ruddy rat-race, the ruddy rush, the ruddy noise, the ruddy everything. They want peace. They want to get back to Mother Earth.'

Thinking perhaps a little dreamily on the subject of Mother Earth, so poetically presented by the Captain, I suddenly thought of something else.

'How large a crew would *The Other Eden* need?'

'I'm hoping to sign on one more hand. Another good strong lass.'

Here I suggested that an all-girl crew might, even in the very best of circumstances, find a voyage of some ten thousand miles a little beyond its powers but Captain Poop-Deck laughed with a most refreshing and persuasive charm.

'Not a bit of it. These girls make damn fine crews. Prefer 'em to men any day. Got more stamina and don't drink so much. In any case we've got Skilly.'

'Who's Skilly?'

'He's the galley boy. Naval man to the core. Cooks like an angel and knows what's best, as naval chaps always do. Worth his weight in gold. Ah! here comes the second round of punches.'

I looked up in the expectation of seeing the blonde bo'sun. Instead, to my great surprise, there appeared at the top of the companion-way a pale, beer-soaked bag of bones in crumpled white shirt and ducks, a torn white pork-pie hat and a slightly blood-stained apron. He looked something like a cross between a galley slave who hadn't seen the light of day for six months and an old lag who had just done a longish stretch in a cellar somewhere. The hand carrying the tray of drinks quivered so much that the glasses tinkled and he stared at me with a trembling, beery eye.

'Ah! good man, Skilly. Got the drinks. Good.'

'Aye, aye, sir.'

'This gentleman here is probably going to join the expedition.'

'Aye, aye, sir. Soon won't have room for 'em all, will we, sir?'

'We damn well won't. It'll probably have to come to a ballot in the end. By the way, what's for supper?'

At this moment I was in the act of picking up my second rum punch from the tray but I could have sworn I saw in the Captain's eye the merest shadow of a wink and an even swifter reflection of it in Skilly's eye.

'Melon, cold salmon mayonnaise, baby new taters, green peas, salads, fresh pineapple and cream, four sorts of cheese and *Other Eden* coffee.'

The Captain, after explaining that *Other Eden* coffee was a speciality laced with rum, said:

'And I daresay a noggin of something too?'

'Aye, aye, sir. I got the 'ock on ice already.'

'Splendid show. Good man. Lay another place for our friend here.'

'Aye, aye, sir.'

Here I was on the point of protesting that I must be on my way when the beery, trembling eyes of Skilly started trembling even more.

'Oh! I pretty near forgot, sir. While you was all having your kip after lunch another young lady called.'

'Good God, man, why didn't you come and wake me? Does she want to join?'

'Aye, aye, sir. Dead keen. Can't wait to get aboard. I told her to come back about seven.'

'Good man, Skilly. Did she say who she was?'

'Lady Sarah somebody, sir, but I can't remember the other bit. She lives in that big house about a couple o' miles up the river.'

Briefly, in silence, I recalled something of the beauties of Lady Sarah. Merely to see her ride past in jodhpurs was to recreate for yourself some of the excitements of Lady Godiva's ride. She sat on horses like a dark goddess. She rode tempestuous races at point-to-points. She was a seductress of other women's husbands. She had once got religion and run away with a rural dean. When she was bored, as she nearly always was, she amused herself by jumping on fresh band-wagons, such as those for nuclear disarmament, banning the bomb or better deals for unmarried mothers. She was sensationally lovely, hopelessly irrepressible, maddeningly dominating and so rich in her own right that she could have shod her hunters with gold.

'I know her,' I said. 'Her father's in whisky.'

The eyes of the Captain positively flamed with vitriolic fire.

'Great guns. Whisky?' He crooked his arm smartly and looked at his watch. 'Blow me down, it's a quarter to seven already. She'll be here any moment now.'

'It rather looks,' I said, 'as if you might complete your crew.'

'Eh? What? Oh! yes.'

Suddenly it seemed to me that the Captain had lost a very great deal of interest in my presence aboard.

'Well, we shall be seeing something of you, I expect. Sorry you can't stay.' Without any other attempt at farewell the Captain turned smartly from me, giving sudden crisp orders. 'Skilly, find the bo'sun. Number One, let's have this deck looking a bit more ship-shape and less like a knacker's yard. At the double.'

I finished my rum punch, climbed unaided down the rope-ladder and started to walk home. About thirty yards down the river bank I turned and looked back at *The Other Eden*. She looked, half-painted, more than a bit ghostly in the declining evening sun, but in imagination I worked on her a momentary transformation.

I seemed to see Lady Sarah, sensational and dominant, as her new figure-head.

A week later I walked back to the boat on a cool, showery afternoon on the chance of having another word with Poop-Deck.

Under the late cloudy August skies the leaves of the poplars above the river banks were full of fretful chatter and beneath them *The Other Eden* presented a sad and surprising sight. She was lying half-submerged, slightly keeled over, in the middle of the river.

While I stared at this melancholy sight, still unable quite to realize that my chance of sharing Captain Poop-Deck's paradise had gone for ever, a dinghy appeared from behind the half-sunken stern. In it was Skilly.

He rowed ashore.

'Hullo, there, Skilly. Salvaging the wreck?'

'Oh! It's you, sir.' He picked up from the bottom of the dinghy a very tired-looking bundle of clothing wrapped in newspaper. He looked more than ever like an old lag starting out on a new life, though not very enthusiastically, after a long stretch. 'Just saving a few duds. All I got in the world.'

'What happened?'

Skilly, dropping the lid of one beery eye, answered with sublime simplicity.

'We was launching her, sir, and she just went down.'

'Somebody pull the plug?'

'Not saying about that, sir.'

'Not the bo'sun by any chance?'

'Not saying about that, sir.'

I stared across at the wreck, thinking once again of my dream of her figure-head.

'Was Lady Sarah aboard at the time?'

'Aye, aye, sir. Very much so, sir. Her and the Captain got as thick as thieves in no time.'

Musing briefly on the appropriateness of this expression I asked if the Captain was about today?

'No, sir. Not about.'

'Any idea where I could get in touch with him?'

'No, sir. No idea. Rather fancy he's gone on a little holiday with Lady Sarah somewhere.'

'And the bo'sun?'

'Couldn't say about her, sir.'

'And Number One?'

'Couldn't say about her either, sir.'

After a short silence Skilly hitched up his drooping bag of bones and looked at me with eyes moist with infinite pleading. I looked back at him with a fairly solemn compassion.

'Haven't got the price of a pint, I suppose, sir?'

I gave him the price of a pint and he touched his cap and said:

'Bless your 'eart, sir. Thanks a lot. May you always have jolly good 'ealth and jolly good luck, sir, and all that.'

'And plenty of melon and salmon mayonnaise and all that.'

'Aye, aye, sir.'

'And fresh pineapple and cream and guavas and breadfruit and the milk of the coconut.'

'Aye, aye, sir. I know what you mean.'

After that I didn't hear of Captain Poop-Deck again for about a year. Then an advertisement in a Sunday paper caught my eye.

It invited you to become a bond-holder in *The Elysian Vineyards Trust*. '*Own your own vines on the very slopes where the Romans grew theirs. Drink your own delicious vintage wine in your own home.*'

The scheme, I discovered, was not only one of entrancing simplicity. It also bore the unmistakable imprint of Poop-Deck. You merely invested in units of twenty-five, fifty, seventy-five or a hundred pounds and in return were allotted an appropriate area of vines. There was no work to do. The staff of trained viticulturalists on the *Elysian Vineyards Trust* did all the work. They bought, planted, pruned and sprayed the vines. They picked, harvested and pressed the grapes. They saw to the fermenting, bottling and dispatching of the wine. A unit of twenty-five pounds would provide you with a bottle of wine every day of the year, a unit of fifty pounds with two bottles per day per year, and all you had to do was stay at home and drink them.

And not only did you sup as the Romans did, on the wines of the Elysian fields. The vines and the good earth on which they grew were yours, without strings, in perpetuity, for ever.

Coconut Radio

ACROSS plates of raw fish, steaming dishes of sucking pig, crabs and liver, fried plantain, curries of prawn and fresh-water shrimp, bowls of bread-fruit, sweet-potatoes and rice, Mr Pilgrim raised his gin glass to me and looked over the edge of it with his pink, under-cooked eyes.

'Those fellows in Africa have the right idea,' he said. 'They're out to keep Africa for the white man.'

'Pass the bread-fruit, Freddy,' Linda said, 'and stop yattering.'

Mr Pilgrim ignored the request for bread-fruit and picked up a rib of sucking pig, warm fat dripping from his fingers. The girl named Linda, splendidly American in rose-coloured shorts, blue silk shirt and a peach-yellow hibiscus in her fair hair, leaned across me, took the bread-fruit dish and said:

'How are you doing? Don't you like bread-fruit? Try some raw fish.'

'Take the Chinks,' Mr Pilgrim said. 'You're interested in people.' He waved the rib of sucking pig at me, dropped it on his plate and picked up another. 'Take the Chinks, now. Here in Tahiti – '

'Anybody ready for wine?' a man said. His name was George. He was tall, with a head like a bald domed white rock and a shirt of orange and purple design that fell outside his copper-coloured trousers. 'Speak up. Take a little wine for thy stomach's sake. Where's Bill Rockley?'

'Entertaining his new *vahini*,' Linda said.

'Who said? Who said? What *vahini* is this?' George said. 'Since when? Who told you?'

'Coconut radio!' a dozen voices said. 'Coconut radio!' Everybody sucked at pig-bones, laughing.

'Anybody seen her? What's she like?' George said. He

moved down the long table of food, pouring red wine into tumblers. 'Gentleman over there, I've forgotten your name. Have some wine? Like the sucking pig? I'm so sorry I've forgotten your name.'

'Matthews.'

'Call him Morgenthau,' a girl said. She was pert, dark, quick-tongued. 'We all call him Morgenthau. He came on the plane with us, didn't you, Morgenthau? He lends us money, don't you, Morgenthau?'

'Well – '

Shyly the young man called Morgenthau, blushing a little, was trying to cut a rib of sucking pig with his knife and fork.

'Saved our lives, Morgenthau did, when the banks weren't open,' the pert, quick-tongued girl said.

'Where are you from, Mr Morgenthau?' Mr Pilgrim asked.

'New Zealand, but – '

'Take the Chinks here,' Mr Pilgrim said. 'You come from a white country, Mr Morgenthau. You don't need to be hit over the head with a sledge-hammer to see which way the wind is blowing, do you?'

'I actually work in Fiji – '

'Another example!' Mr Pilgrim said. 'Worse if anything. Take the Indians in Fiji – '

'I wonder where Bill Rockley is?' Linda said. 'Bill is fun. I miss Bill.'

'He'll be here,' George said. 'He knows about the sucking pig. Come to that, where's that man of yours? Where's Henry?'

'Must you ask?' she said. 'Somewhere between here and Bora-Bora. As usual. With that damned out-board put-put. Catching tuna. One day a shark – '

'Reminds me,' a man said. He was hairy-chested, but otherwise bald too. His open shirt was sulphur yellow, with a design of green sword-fish across it. His slacks were pale blue, the top buttons of the front undone, letting his paunch protrude.

Beside him sat a thin, blank-eyed Tahitian girl drinking gin. She did not, I noticed, eat very much. Sometimes she took up a rib of sucking pig, held it absent-eyed for a time in her fingers and then, equally absent-eyed, gave it to the man beside her. She did not look young and the listless skin of her face, something the colour of old, faded straw, was deeply pock-marked.

'Reminds you of what?' George said. 'Don't be so damned secretive. Don't feed the animal, Marcelle, if he won't talk.'

The girl, Marcelle, did not smile.

'I hear the new *vahini* comes from Bora-Bora, that's all. I don't know, I just heard – '

'Where from? Who said?'

'Coconut radio again!' they all said. 'Coconut radio!'

'Everywhere this same pattern,' Mr Pilgrim said to me, 'is manifesting itself. Have some raw fish? Try the shrimps – the shrimps are delicious. Take the Indians in Fiji. Eh, Mr Morgenthau, you know all about the Indians in Fiji. What were they, fifty, sixty years ago?'

'Coolies mostly. Indentured labour – '

'Exactly. And what are they now? Rich. Prosperous. Prolific as flies. Outnumbering everybody.' He helped himself to large portions of raw fish and curried prawns. 'And the Chinks. Take the Chinks. Not only here in Tahiti, but in Honolulu. In San Francisco. And the Japs. Take the Japs in San Francisco. Three generations back – '

'How long have you been here, Mr Morgenthau?' a voice said. 'Your first visit?'

'Well, just – '

Mr Morgenthau blushed, still trying to cut ribs of sucking pig with his knife and fork, and looked mildly and shyly about him.

'Mr Morgenthau's too wild!' someone said. 'He needs taming. Can't we get him a *vahini*? What about it, Mr Morgenthau? Stay here and settle down and pick yourself a nice *vahini*.'

'What exactly,' Mr Morgenthau said, 'is a *vahini?*'

Mr Pilgrim, who was now cracking crabs' claws, took advantage of the rising gust of laughter to turn round, screen his mouth with one arm and address me confidentially.

'You know, I suppose, that among themselves they are largely infertile?' he said. 'You appreciate that?'

'No, I hadn't –'

'The Tahitians I mean. These girls. With whites, even with Chinese, right as rain.' Already very flushed, his eyes cooked to a deeper, moister pink, he reached out, took up a bottle and poured himself more wine. 'But among themselves – phut!'

'If Bill doesn't hurry soon,' someone said, 'there'll be no more sucking pig.'

'The real truth is of course,' Mr Pilgrim said, and again he addressed me confidentially, cracking a crab's claw, 'that the whole place is ruined. Travesty. You hear all this talk about the paradise? The paradise has gone, old boy. It's finished. They've ruined it completely.'

'You mean the whites?'

'Not the whites. Good God, the French.'

Large dishes of glowing water-melon, frosty-pink, came down the table, followed by pineapple, banana and passion-fruit. Mr Pilgrim, though not yet finished with crabs, chose a passion-fruit and began to press it to his lips, giving it quick sucking kisses.

'How do they strike you?' he said. 'What's your honest opinion? Looks, I mean.'

'Some are nice.'

'But on the whole? Disappointing, wouldn't you say?'

'Not disappointing,' I said. 'Only lost. Only very sad.'

'Sad? Perhaps you're right,' Mr Pilgrim said. He sucked loudly at his fruit. 'Though that doesn't alter –'

'Bill!' someone shouted. 'Bill!' everyone began to say. 'Bill! Where were you? What happened? Don't tell! – we know. Everybody knows –'

'Can't a man keep anything to himself? – '

'Coconut radio again!' they all shouted. 'Coconut radio!'

'For those who don't know this fellow already,' George said, 'this is Bill Rockley.'

A sombre, tallish man, brown, dark-haired, looking a little more than forty, smiled down the table and said, 'Hullo' several times. His shirt was blue-black check and this, perhaps, together with a dark moustache, made him seem older than he was.

'Like to introduce Michele to everybody,' he said. 'Everybody – Michele.'

The girl who stood beside him smiled down at us with wide dark eyes. Her hair was plaited. It fell over her bare shoulders in two thick blue-black ropes, reaching below her hips. She was perhaps fourteen or fifteen and under the vermilion hibiscus-pattern of her pereu her breasts were beautiful, taut and high. With shyness and grace she stood with one knee gently overlapping the other, one hand fingering the yellow hibiscus in her hair.

'Fine!' George said. 'Get the man some sucking pig.'

Grinning rinds of melon were now littered about the table. Mr Pilgrim helped himself to another passion fruit. The shy Mr Morgenthau fingered the last of his pig's bones. Mr Pilgrim, unable to focus his reddening eyes correctly on the passion fruit, bit it at one edge, squirting juice, flesh and seeds down his chin. And then, as music suddenly flooded about the room, the pert, dark, quick-tongued girl laughed and shouted:

'Good, a record. Marvellous. I love that tune. I adore that Tahitian tune. Isn't somebody going to dance? Mr Pilgrim, dance with me!'

Mr Pilgrim, his chin still covered with passion fruit, staggered to his feet for dancing.

'Good idea!' Linda said. 'Morgenthau! Dance with me! Lend me your arms!'

Soon everybody was dancing. Even the shy Mr Morgenthau was dancing.

Only the girl with the yellow hibiscus in her hair and myself were left at the table, staring at the wreckage of pigs' ribs, the grinning rinds of melon, the crabs and their claws.

MORE ABOUT PENGUINS

Penguin Book News, which appears every month, contains details of all the new books issued by Penguins as they are published. From time to time it is supplemented by *Penguins in Print* – a complete list of all our available titles. (There are well over three thousand of these.)

A specimen copy of *Penguin Book News* will be sent to you free on request, and you can become a subscriber for the price of the postage – 4s for a year's issues (including the complete lists). Just write to Dept EP, Penguin Books Ltd, Harmondsworth, Middlesex, enclosing a cheque or postal order, and your name will be added to the mailing list.

Some other Penguins by H. E. Bates are described on the following pages.

Note: *Penguin Book News* and *Penguins in Print* are not available in the U.S.A. or Canada

Also by H. E. Bates

Fair Stood the Wind for France

'Perhaps the finest novel of the war ... The scenes
are exquisitely done and the characters – tenderly
and beautifully drawn – are an epitome of all that is
best in the youth of the two countries. This is a
fine, lovely book which makes the heart beat with
pride' – *Daily Telegraph*

A Moment in Time

She was still in her teens when they came to fight a
war in the air. Day by precarious day she shared
with these dedicated youngsters – hardly more than
boys – dangers unbearably heightened by the
peace of the English countryside.

Not for sale in the U.S.A.